INDYGOS SAGA: THE ALPHA & THE OMEGA

Indygos Saga: The Alpha & The Omega

The Alpha and the Omega

P. WILSON

P. Wilson

CONTENTS

CONTENTS

COPYRIGHT

PREFACE

I was given a second chance at life. After my re-birth, I was given new eyes, new ears, and a new mind. All of which became unsatisfied with the daily routine of things, which led to a plague of questions that formed in my mind. Waking up daily with these questions then turned into a series of actions becoming necessary to divide who I was from who I am.

The division of past and present created an awareness within me I did not know was there, an awareness I did not realize would cost me so much... It then became important to me to share my journey with others, so that they may also open their minds to the possibilities and mysteries of life, which led to the creation of the Indygos Saga.

This saga is about a group of individuals, known as the Indygos, that operate in a reciprocal relationship with the divine Universal Subconscious Mind; the mechanics of the relationship being established before birth. The divine Universal Subconscious Mind shares its knowledge, insight, wisdom, and guidance, with the enlightened individual, to pass along to humanity; awakening humanity from its somber.

There are many truths concealed from us, however, the hunger for wisdom and truth always prevails in the end. Once this connection is sought and attained, it becomes life-changing on every plane. It accesses barriers within the mind previously unreached and forces change, ultimately creating a revolution of life changing events. All of which are created by planting seeds that inspire and encourage truth and realization of them.

The first book of Indygos Saga takes you to the very beginning. It is the story of a woman who changed the world with a single thought. A thought that led to a series of actions, taken over time that produced revolutionary changes that were felt across the world, inspiring millions of others. In this life, one should never underestimate the power of thoughts, because those thoughts become things, tangible things!

Your thoughts then become your words, which then become your actions. The series of actions you take, then become your destiny. Your destiny creates the legacy you leave behind; or, in some cases, serves as breadcrumbs you leave behind from one life you live to another you will live in the future.

We, the Indygos, were always here. We have always been here, and will always be here. We come in many forms and variations; here to spread the way, the truth, and the light. There are many evils that hides in plain sight. It is up to us, the Indygos, to lift the veil that disguises the evils.

In exposing these various evils; we are protecting and ensuring freedom and safety while establishing a new way and a new life. Too often we are told lies and believe them. We are fed bullshit propaganda, then told how we are to think, speak, feel, act, and do. Everything we have ever been told is all an attempt to control us and steal the one thing we can never get back...

Time.

ACKNOWLEDGMENTS

My children and family are, always have been, and always will be my source of pure creativity and inspiration. I love you all, always. Continue letting your lights shine!

~ 1 ~

CHAPTER ONE:

The Beginning

Hindsight is always 20/20. We never seem to see the significance of some things until confronted with the inevitable consequences and outcomes plausible to the situation(s), and/or people at hand.

However, there comes a point in time in life when intuition kicks in; no longer using reasoning with emotions and logic alone. We begin using a connection to something deeper. This deeper connection then takes us to the inevitable endpoints, no matter which path we take.

All roads lead to home.

Become who you are.

I woke up in a completely dark room; just a few blinking red and green lights. I could hear faint mumbling in the background but had no idea where I was. *Where was I and how in the hell did I end up here?!* I thought to myself. Suddenly, my memories started flooding back to me slowly; creating a pit in my stomach. *What have I done?*

Too many things had gone wrong suddenly, without a single calculation being made. Yet I was a skilled tactician (or at least I thought I was). Hell, I mitigated multi-million-dollar risks for a living but clearly made a severe miscalculation within my steps that put me here. Miscalculations that could have taken everything from me. Miscalculations that were not miscalculations at all, but rather calculations that never happened to begin with.

I looked around trying to figure out where I was. I was hooked up to an IV and appeared to be in a hospital. I turned to my side, looked out the window, and saw a parking lot full of cars; there were a lot of bright blinking lights with arrows, indicating where to park. I scanned the darkroom frantically for the nearest exit to make a mad dash out of there.

As I lay there retracing my last steps and planning my escape; I remember grabbing drinks with coworkers after work for happy hour, but cannot seem to recall anything after that. I was never much of a drinker, but I could handle a drink or two with plenty of water. I remember sticking to my two-drink limit and drunk plenty of water. *What happened?!* I kept trying to recall the details but was unable.

A sudden crashing thought came to me about my two children at home I needed to get back to. They have no one else here in this state or remotely close to it, but me. *How could I be so stupid?!* I thought to myself. In a frantic rush, I reached over, ripped my IV out, got out of bed, and took two steps forward. A rush of blood flowed down my arm from where I ripped my IV out, I tried putting my hand over the wound but the blood would not stop and continued gushing through my fingers.

By this time, I had set off alarms in the hospital by removing my vital scanners, and a nurse rushed into the room.

"Oh my God, you came back to us! I did not think you were going to make it! You are a miracle!"

I just stared at her blankly and began to explain that I have two children at home by themselves right now - probably worried about where their mother is and that I needed to get back home. In a low voice, she told me I would not be able to leave right now and helped me over to the mirror. She gave warning to prepare myself for the light. I listened to her instruction, anxiously awaiting to see what the damage was.

As the light came on, all I could do was gasp. My face, or what used to be my face, was completely unrecognizable. As I gazed at myself in the mirror, I could feel my knees getting weak and started feeling like I was going to pass out from what I had just seen. I forced myself to stand a little longer to take in the damage I had done. My entire face was swollen with a multi-colored hematoma on the left corner of my forehead that was the size of a baseball.

My right eyelid was hanging by tiny shreds of skin, leaving behind a gaping hole where my eyelid used to be. My left arm was severely burned with bloody pieces of missing skin all over. There was an annoying pain that kept radiating up through my left leg. I have never had a broken bone before, but I assumed it had to be broken due to this irritant of a radiating pain that ceaselessly sent continuous shocks of pain up my left leg.

This was too much to take in. Suddenly, that weak feeling came rushing back, then everything went black. I woke up several hours later in a new room but was left in the same bad dream. I thought to myself, *how the hell is this possible?!! Why do I keep coming back to this nightmare?! This nightmare is horrible and I must wake up!! In real life, I would have never allowed myself to be in this kind of a position! This is reckless and nothing like me!*

I lie still for a moment and thought back to what I saw the last time I woke up in this nightmare. I thought to myself, *if you go look in the mirror and you see the same messed up face, then you know this is real and shit just got really real.* I figured if this dream is reality, it is probably not the best idea to rip out my IV again, considering the amount of blood I lost the last time. I slid my legs around the bed, grabbed my IV machine, and carried it over to the mirror with me.

As I hobbled over to the mirror, I felt that same irritating shocking pain radiating up through my left leg like the last time I got out of bed. *Hmm...,* I thought to myself. *If this is a bad dream, I can note the same pain in the same leg, as the last time.* Once I got in front of the mirror, I stood there in horror and just froze.

I could not move at all. It was almost as if something supernatural was holding me there, forcing me to take in my mistakes of horror. I felt a tear fall from my left eye, followed by the full fledge of waterworks. I could no longer even recognize myself anymore; I was no longer who I once was. I was a monster now!

I could not look any longer and made my way back to the bed and sat down. I began staring out the window, numb and unable to move, think, or speak. As I looked out the window trying to remember anything about what happened, I remembered seeing my grandmother.

She was sitting on a wooden swing that was attached to this enormous tree I was laying under. I was very close to my grandma, growing up. She was one, of the very few, I could depend on, throughout my life. But a few months ago, she passed away. Her passing figuratively and literally, killed me. The months before her passing was the most unbearable of them all.

When I lost her, I lost a big piece of myself too. On top of going through a long and drawn-out divorce that lingered for over a year; I also had to bury one of the only people who ever loved and cared about me. Everything became too much to process and darkness settled in.

As I sat there, continuing in that thought, I went back to that memory of my grandma sitting on that wooden swing. I was laying in tall, bladed grass that felt like pillows, not like any of the grass I was used to. Staring up at the sun in awe, wanting to go there as if it were a reachable destination. It was so warm wherever that was, and I just felt so comfy, cozy.

It reminded me of how I felt when I used to curl up in my PJs with a cup of hot cocoa in front of my fireplace with a blanket and a book. That warmth was unlike anything I have ever experienced. It was like I was placed inside of something that projected a constant warm temperature. This place was also able to project all the associated feelings of warmth - like safety, protection, love, and so much more.

In front of my feet was the most beautiful river that was unlike anything I had ever seen. The water was just there, not moving; there was no flow, waves, or currents, but had the most crystal-clear, blue water. The way the sun sparkled all over it put you into a trance of peace and tranquility.

My hair was longer and my curls shined like strands made of pure golden-brown honey. I remembered raising my hands, looking at them as the beams of sunlight shone through my fingers. As the desire became stronger to navigate toward the sun, I could feel my body begin to lift from the grassy area I was laying in. As I started rising in the air, my grandmother looked back at me from the wooden swing she was sitting on and said,

"It's not your time."

Her words took flight from my body, laying me back down in the soft, pillowy grass. I snapped out of my thoughts and back into the current reality here in this hospital room I was in. My heart broke into a million pieces. I could not tell what was real and what was a dream anymore.

However, I knew this current version of reality I was experiencing was not the dream state I was once in. It was real, and what I had gotten myself into was even more real! I thought to myself about the two options I left myself with. The first option being me playing the victim - feeling sorry for myself and going on about how I should not be here.

Or the second option being to accept my fuck up, allowing no self-pity - and to rectify the situation no matter what it took. I have never been one to play victim, and that was not about to start now. I have come too far and have been through too much to go out like some kind of victim, especially a victim of my own making.

Even though I was at an incredibly weak point in my life, I chose to see it as another incredibly strong turning point in my life. I went with option two and looked around the room for a phone. My purse and cell were nowhere in sight and the phone in the hospital room had no dial tone to reach an outside line. Just when I could feel the blood rushing to my face in panic, a familiar face walked into my room.

"I'm happy you're awake and came back to us," the nurse said.

"What happened to me?" I asked. She replied with words I will never forget for the rest of my life.

"You are a miracle, that's what happened to you!"

"Why are you saying this though, what happened? Where is my truck and purse?" I asked, confused and anxious.

"I am saying this because you are a miracle! There is no medical explanation for how you survived the accident you just had. You were brought back to life twice, once in the ambulance and another time here. Your coordinates were sent to the police by your car alerting us to the SOS.

"Seeing how all of that happened, and you are still here; I am not sure what you consider a miracle to be, but to us here, you are the very definition of a miracle! As for your truck, I do not know, but I put your purse in a locker in the back. I will be right back, let me go and find you a hospital phone that works."

I had no words. I mean, on one hand, I understood I should be happy about being a miracle, but, if she experienced what I just experienced, she would understand my current disappointment. Once she returned with the phone and hooked it up, I asked how long I was going to have to stay in the hospital.

Laughing, she said, "Honey, you are in the intensive care unit and you need emergency eye surgery, you are going to be here for a while. I will come back to check on you in a few minutes to give you some time to make your calls."

I sat there and thought about what she just said – *"a while"?? Oh, hell no! I cannot stay here for a while; we are going to have to have a serious discussion about this once she gets back here! I mean...what does "a while" even mean?! A few days, weeks, months; and why?!*

My thoughts were racing all over the place! Panic was setting in. I did not have "a while" to give. I began trying to remember the phone numbers to my house, my kid's cell phones, but no matter how hard I tried, I could not remember them. The only phone numbers I could seem to remember were my ex-husband's and my questionable friend, Jenayah.

Going with the lesser of two evils, I frantically typed in Jenayah's phone number and could hear ringing.

"Hello?"

Immediate relief hit my body the moment she answered. It was as if I somehow knew everything was going to be okay.

"Hey, it's me."

"Cam?! Are you okay?! We have been trying to reach you for several hours! Where are you?"

I could hear the anxiety in her voice and this time, there was absolutely nothing I could do or say to put it at rest. The "we have" part meant my kids are looking for me too.

"I fucked up and I need you to get here now, please!" That is all I could manage to get out.

"Looking up flights now to get to you. Is anybody there with the kids right now?"

I hated the fact that I had to respond with no, but I had to put my pride aside and get help there with them as soon as possible. As I responded to her with "no," the waterworks started again and this time I could not turn them off.

"Do not worry, I will be there by 6 am this morning. I am getting a bag ready now and will go there and get them the moment I land."

I was so thankful for her at this moment, all our bullshit to the side. I got my home phone number from her before hanging up with her, and then called home. After my calls went to voicemail a few times, Emanii finally answered.

"Hello?"

"It's me," I replied.

"Mommy?!" I could hear the sadness instantly on the other side of the phone.

"Yes baby, it's me." All I felt was sheer disgust toward myself for making my innocent children feel this way.

"What happened?!"

"I made a disastrous mistake and... I was in a bad car accident. I am in the hospital right now and have to go through a little surgery, but, please do not worry. I am okay, I promise. How is your brother doing?"

"Oh my gosh!! I knew something bad happened! I called both Jenayah and grandma and neither one of them knew where you were either. Once your phone started going straight to voicemail, I started praying because something was telling me this is not good! I am just so thankful you are alive! King fell asleep, I think – I can check?"

"No, let him sleep. You go to sleep too, if you can. Jenayah will be there first thing in the morning to get you guys. Please do not worry, I am okay. I love you very much and will see you soon."

"Okay, I am just so happy you are okay and that you are alive, Mommy. I love you too and I will see you soon."

As I hung up the phone, I thought back over my life, or what I could remember of it. I allowed my misguided judgments and emotions to almost take the things I care about the most away from me. I swore to myself at this moment I would never allow anything like this to ever happen again. Nothing at that moment could ever or will ever take away the helplessness I felt at this exact moment.

I made one more brief call to let my boss know what was going on and that I would more than likely not be returning to work that following Monday. A little while later, the nurse was back with a doctor who examined my eye and took me back for the emergency surgery to fix my eyelid.

After surgery, I woke up in my room with both of my beautiful children and my only friend at my side. I was so thankful to be able to see, touch, and be in the presence of my children again. This is a moment I would never forget because it was purest, most unconditional love I had ever felt.

They both saw me in my rawest, most real, and weak form. I was completely open and exposed, and they never judged me, not once. Even with all my newfound hideousness, they still fully embraced me, accepting me for exactly who I was; allowing me the room to make mistakes too.

I did not want to hide my pain from them anymore, I was no longer ashamed of the things I had gone through. I took pride in knowing that I would get past these things, not allowing myself to get stuck in bondage by them. I fucked up royally, but I also owned that fuck up 110%. I did not want to make excuses for any of it and had a deep intrinsic knowing that things were going to change on every level of my life.

Life as I knew it would no longer be the same. My children would no longer be the same. I would no longer be the same... The next few days I spent drifting in and out of consciousness. I had so many different doctors coming in and out of my room all the time and throughout all times in the morning and night.

Each panel of doctors with the same questions and the same "miracle" response. They would check on my burns, the cuts on my face, body, and arm, and examine my broken leg. I was taken back for several CAT scans and sometimes would have to go back for additional ones of my entire body. It was exhausting and I felt like a lab rat that was constantly under observation.

I realized the severity of my accident but did not quite understand the frequency of visits from the doctors and nurses, nor the reason I was still in the ICU. With almost every one of their visits, I could almost count on something being put into my IV, putting me right back to sleep.

*****

This time as I fell asleep, I was brought back to the grassy area by the still water from my accident. I saw my grandmother sitting on that same wooden swing again, but she was smiling now, unlike after my accident. As I turned to look at what she was smiling at, I saw a beautiful little girl sitting by the still water lake.

The little girl was sitting down by the lake with her feet in the crystal-clear, blue water. I could not see her face, her back was facing me, with her face toward the sun. She had long, sandy-brown, super curly hair that glistened like pieces of gold against the sunlight. Not knowing who this little visitor was, I decided I would go over and join her at the lake and introduce myself.

As I placed my feet into the water next to her, I felt a sense of pure relaxation and healing melt into my body. It was as if I was being cleaned and healed at the same time. The feeling is truly hard to put into words, but I felt completely purified.

"I brought you here to warn you," said the little girl, softly.

"Well, that is one hell of a greeting! Warn me of what?" I replied, thrown off by her warning.

"The place you currently are keeps people sick and creates dependents; it cannot provide the healing you require. Their work with you is complete. They completed the exact tasks they were supposed to. You, now, must release yourself from this place, you are not a prisoner nor are you a victim."

"Who are you?" I asked.

"You know who I am, silly. It is time to go home."

*****

Just like that, I was back awake. I sat up in my hospital bed, looking over at my children who were asleep on the hospital chairs next to my bed. The more I thought about what the little girl said, the more I could see what she was saying. I thought to myself, *why was I still in this hospital?!*

My eyelid was stitched back together and my leg is not going into a cast - it will heal on its own, along with the cuts and burns. I started thinking back and ever since I was a little girl, I have always hated hospitals. They smell weird and every time I had to go to one, it was usually to see someone either about to pass away or who did pass away. I wanted out of this place, right now! I paged the nurse to bring her to my room, and a few moments later she returned.

"Seriously, why am I still here?" I asked my nurse. "My eye is fixed now and my leg is not going in a cast. My cuts and burns will heal on their own. Please let me go home, I miss my cat, my bed, and my home. My kids need to be back home too."

She began laughing, which was becoming her normal response to me. "I cannot release you without orders from the doctor, honey... We need to monitor you and make sure nothing major happens. Sometimes, in severe trauma patient cases, new symptoms pop up that need immediate treatment.

"We would not want to release you and have something happen that could cost time and ultimately, your life. You need to give it some time to heal. Please, just lay back down. You cannot rush healing honey..."

Three days later, I was still in the ICU. I was getting constant meds put into my IV with a new panel of doctors coming in every couple of hours. By the fourth day, I had more than enough of the bullshit and was done being the lab rat of constant observation. I woke up and paged the nurse on duty and to my surprise, I had a new nurse.

Once she came into my room, I explained how I wanted to be released, but was told, yet again, about how I could not be released without the doctor's orders. With my frustration level reaching an all-time high, I demanded to be released and wanted to speak with the doctor on duty directly. I did not want to continue arguing with someone about something that was not within their control. When she finished taking my vitals, she told me she would return with the doctor.

Several hours later, the doctor came in. I explained my demands and, shockingly, to my surprise, the doctor did not even argue and was willing to release me. Within a few more hours, the nurse came back to my room with my discharge papers and some pain medicine prescriptions. Just like that, they released me from the hospital, and could go home. I felt so liberated and free, like a brand-new woman!

During the drive home, I noticed everything looked different and more defined. The colors appeared much more vibrant with certain colors hurting my eyes to look at. Sounds were much clearer; audible with a filter that allowed me to hear every single sound, removing and filtering out the different background noises.

I took a drink of the apple juice I brought with me from the hospital and noticed my taste was intensified. I could taste each of the different variations of apples that were blended to make this specific bottle of juice. Along with the water that cleansed the apples and the plastic that housed the juice within it. Everything was beautiful. Everything was new. It was as if it were my first time seeing, hearing, smelling, and tasting.

Thinking back to where I just left, it was all like a terrible nightmare I could not wake up from. There were so many things I did not understand and so many questions I had. The more I thought about those questions, the more furious I became. With this fury, came a rising of anger. A rising of anger I had never felt before on this level before. Anger that was birthed from the death and the pain, and now, the resurrection.

I do not remember a single thing that was talked about on the ride home. Somewhere along the ride I completely blanked out, getting lost in all translation. The moment I walked into my little apartment, I could not take it anymore and burst into tears. I was terrified of being left alone, again, and more than anything, I was terrified of not knowing who I was any longer.

I knew deep inside that who I used to know as Camryn Wolf, died on April 25, 2019, at 8:19 pm, EST, and there was nothing and no one that could bring her back. I killed her and now I was left with the eerie hauntings of my mistakes. This new person, this unknown entity that was taking my body over; this was the part that scared me the most. Being alone with this new person, this unknown entity, made me realize I was embarking in new territory. Territory I had never charted before.

I was not sure what would become of this new entity and how I was to integrate it into my life. The only thing I could do was cry, there was no way to put into words exactly what I was feeling. The knowing I would be forced to be alone with this entity. Forced to chart this new territory together with a force I had no understanding of. Forced to begin again as a new Cam. One I hardly recognized anymore.

~ 2 ~

CHAPTER TWO:

Reality Check

The saying goes that the grass is not greener on the other side, but I have never agreed nor understood that statement. The grass is always greener where it is cared for and watered properly.

We work the same way as every other living organism - light being the bearer of shape and life, dark being the bearer of death and transformation.

Reality stands in the middle as a test of our landscape; holding a testament to the fruits of our labors.

Sometimes we think we have everything figured out, just to find out we knew nothing at all. I did not know who I was anymore or what anything meant. There were so many things that made little sense to me and the more I thought about it, the madder I got at God. I thought to myself, *how could you bring me back here to this place?! You show me the most beautiful, peaceful, and calming place and allow me to keep the memory of it but refused to allow me to stay?! WHY?!!!!*

I was pissed off! No, I was more than pissed off, I was infuriated! Absolutely nothing of this situation made sense to me, and I craved understanding, more than anything. With that craving for understanding came feelings of hopelessness, despair, and confusion. But this is when everything started to change.

At this moment, it dawned on me that I could either become more of what I already was, or from my ashes, I could recreate myself. Evolving into who I am to become. I chose the second option, again, reinforcing my "take ownership" attitude in the hospital. I came to the conclusion that the next moves I would make would establish who I am now and there was no point in looking back at the past because I no longer resided there.

I had no clue where to start or begin, so I decided to go back to the beginning and went to the place that was holding my truck. I needed to see, in the physical, what happened that night and try to retrace my steps. I had no memory of what happened but it was my hope that the evidence within my truck would hold at least some of the answers.

As Jenayah and I pulled up to the tow site, I could feel the inside of me becoming drained and weak. Almost as if I was getting closer to some kind of source that was capable of physically taking my energy from me. I did not care and would not allow this to stop me. This is something I had to do, no matter the cost. I needed answers.

I faced my fears, even though I was very much so afraid. I opened the car door and began slowing hobbling my way up to the door. A man then came out before I could reach the door and asked me if I was the owner of the black BMW X3 truck that was brought in a couple of days ago. I am not sure how he was able to guess this truck belonged to me but assumed it was due to my new monstrous appearance I had taken on a few days ago.

When I confirmed I was the owner, he told me to follow him back to where my truck was parked. My truck was unrecognizable, like my face when I first woke up in the hospital. I slowly approached the vehicle from behind. The first thing I noticed was the entire passenger side of the truck was completely smashed in. The back passenger door was missing the trim and the trim on the front passenger door was dangling by a few pieces of metal.

Tree debris stuck out of the front passenger tire and various other areas of the truck. The front passenger window was demolished. Looking inside the truck, I could see the deployed airbags still hanging out of the dash and sides. I slowly moved around to the front of the vehicle and the windshield was still intact, but was shattered into a million tiny little pieces, except directly in front of the driver's side.

For some reason, the driver's side looked completely untouched. The hood of the truck was smashed up to the windshield with all major components exposed, also covered in tree debris that hung out from various places. As I walked around to the driver's door, I felt that draining energy source becoming stronger, making me feel even weaker. I grabbed onto my truck for leverage, continuing to make my way to the driver's door.

When I finally made it over to the driver's side, what immediately stood out to me was the driver's door window. The window was missing, there were no glass fragments on the seat or the floor. As the man was beginning to walk away, I asked him,

"Where is the driver's door window?"

He replied, "We tried looking for it and could not find it. It was nowhere near the accident scene or inside the truck. It looked as if someone plucked the window straight out of the truck door. It doesn't look like a window was ever there."

The moment he spoke those words, I could feel a chill spread up my spine and into my scalp. I turned around to continue examining the inside of the truck and the mystery astonished me. The damage was astounding, I was left mystified as to how anyone could have possibly made it out of this alive. I looked around in complete sadness and stood there for a moment, unable to move, paralyzed in terror.

I realized that if I had someone in that passenger seat with me, that would have been the last ride they ever took. As I walked around to the back of the truck, I noticed the back was smashed up too! Unclear how this could have possibly happened and unable to fight the tears any longer, I fell to my knees and cried.

I felt like the wind had been knocked right out of me! I could not believe what I was seeing, but even more so, I could not believe what I had just lived through; walking away with minor injuries (comparatively speaking). Jenayah came over to me and helped me to my feet. We walked back to her rental car in complete silence.

She then went back to the truck, began taking pictures, and then proceeded to pack up my belongings that were still in the truck. She put those items into a bag for me to go through later, when ready. The ride back home was silent. I had no words, only pain. Jenayah also sat in silence, crying with me. I think we were both in complete shock. I did not find any answers, only more hopelessness. In my mind, seeing my truck would allow me to retrace my steps. However, I ended up walking away with more questions than answers.

Seeing myself after the accident was nothing compared to seeing my truck. I did not understand how I walked away from this alive. As I looked at the pictures Jenayah took of my totaled truck, I thought more about what the guy at the tow place said about the driver's door glass being plucked. As I kept staring at the pictures of my windshield, I became much more perplexed.

The pictures looked like someone or something entered my truck upon me colliding with the tree, and threw me from my driver's door window. There is no way this someone or something could have been human. Thinking about this logically, there is no possible way to enter another vehicle moments before a crash and strategically remove the driver's door glass.

Leaving behind no trace, and then somehow managing to throw me through the door, moments before colliding with a tree. Whatever saved me was not human. It was something else, something or someone outside of any logic and reason. Whoever and whatever saved me was now connected to me. To what capacity, I was unsure. But deep inside I knew the events from the accident solidified this mysterious connection through blood.

Things were changing inside of me. My perceptions, my belief system, my tolerance for things, along with all my senses becoming heightened. I felt everything yet nothing at all. But most of all, I felt utterly lost. I laid in bed that night staring at the pictures of my truck, trying to make sense of it all. But no matter how hard I tried, I still could not remember what exactly happened to me that night of the accident.

It was as if a memory wipe or some kind of block was put on my mind; blocking me from retrieving this information. The more I tried to remember what happened, the more exhausted it left me. I went to bed that night and drifted off to sleep instantly, completely exhausted from the events of today.

*****

Entering my dream state, the little girl came to visit me again. She was wearing a veil that covered her face, and she spoke no words. We were not at the grassy area I usually came to, when entering my dream state. This time, I arrived somewhere completely different.

We were right outside of a big beautiful house that was all white with black shutters. The house was well lit with soft lights surrounding the entrance to the home. The entrance of the home was surrounded by a bronze gate that had the name "Wolf" engraved on a plate at the top of the fence. The little girl opened her hand toward me.

"Take my hand, I want to show you something," she said.

I put my hand in hers, and as I did the gates to the home opened. We began walking toward the entrance. Directly in front of the entrance, there was a huge water fountain in the middle of the big, open, grassy area, that formed a circle.

The water fountain was a beautiful statue of a goddess angel with wings that were spread out. One wing was white, and the other was black. The goddess angel held within her hands a vividly colored marble that resembled the earth; from which water poured into a brightly lit open well. The open well was shallow and housed many bright neon fish in it.

The goddess had a crown atop her head that was also brightly lit and had the brightest emerald jewel in the center of it. I was impressed with the details of this monument but wondered what it all meant. Someone with this much attention to detail certainly has a meaning or multiple meanings, for a statue like this.

As we made our way to the front door, I looked up and noticed the wrap-around balconies that went along the upper and lower decks of the home. The balconies created this halo effect that wrapped around the entire house. When we approached the door, the little girl asked if I was ready to go in. As I put my hand her in hers for confirmation, the door began to opened automatically for us to enter.

The inside of this home was just as beautiful and extremely detailed just like it was outside. There were high ceilings with double crown molds, elegant fixtures made of bronze, ceiling to floor curtains, and vases of white flowers everywhere. An enormous library, was straight ahead of the entrance door that had ceiling to floor book cases filled with a vast multitude of books. Fiction, non-fiction, magazines, newspapers, and alike.

I made my way over to the kitchen and looked out the window. It captured the most beautiful view of the Atlantic Ocean I had ever seen. When suddenly, I could hear voices outside. I made my way out to the patio area where the voices were coming from. As I made my way out to the patio, I saw my children and I with an old high school friend of mine I had not seen or talked to in years.

We were all laughing and appeared so happy! It looked as if we were about to head out on a boat adventure, as I could see bags being put onto a boat that was docked in the docking area nearby. On my left hand, I could see that I was wearing a HUGE rock on my wedding ring finger. Confused at what I was looking at, I turned and asked the little girl,

"What is the purpose of what you are showing me? What does this mean? Is this real?"

The little girl replied, "At the end of what I show you, you will understand everything, I promise. If not, I will help you under-stand."

I shook my head in understanding and continued to observe as an outsider. Once the bags and other items were placed in the boat, we came to sit down at the patio table. The outside patio table was circular and made of white and gray stones. There was a pink, blue, and white 6-wick candle burning, that sat centered on a beautiful square glass tray that was surrounded by different colored seashells.

The patio seating area was nestled in a nook that had greenery above it and to the sides of it. A white crisscross arch entryway led to an infinity pool and hot tub area that was softly lit. It was a sight for sore eyes, especially mine. The little girl and I made our way back inside the house, where she gave me a brief tour of each of the rooms in the house.

Time was then fast-forwarded to show how my life played out. I owned a chain of successful businesses in Miami, Florida. Emanii was a successful architect/engineer of a firm she built herself, and King was a successful basketball player. I got a sense of abundant love that surrounded us, with me appearing to be a leader of something I was yet to understand.

The way this version of myself conducted herself through business, finances, and my children, differed from how I currently handled things. This version displayed inner knowing and unshakable confidence that was shown through my voice and gestures. I never appeared to show uncertainty, doubt, or any kind of weakness. This version was bold and courageous, yet, gentle, loving, and patient.

In an instant, we arrived at another home. This home was not well lit and did not appear to be cared for like the previous home we just left. This home was nestled within a planned unit development (PUD), along with multiple other homes that went along the same road and were placed closely together. The outside of the home was pale tan with white shutters and edges.

The home was surrounded by a tall white fence with wilted and dead-looking grass all around the home. It did not seem like anyone was living there. The little girl looked turned to me and asked me if I was ready to go inside and as I said yes, the door opened at my command. The energy in this home was completely different from the first one she took me to.

Upon walking in, I could tell the inside of the home was cared for, unlike the outside, but still felt empty. There was a white partition with green vines separating the foyer from the office that was on the other side. The office had a big white desk with three monitors, a laptop, a phone, and a printer.

As we walked through the kitchen, I looked through the glass patio doors and saw the backyard area had a pool. But, the enclosure around the pool was torn up and tattered. The pool did not look like anyone went swimming in there in months. The home was quiet, increasing my suspense to locate where everyone was.

We began to head up the stairs and into the loft area. There was another desk with a few monitors and a laptop. I was sitting there at the desk working and looked miserable. I wasn't sure what happened to this version of myself, but I had lost a lot of weight and appeared to drown myself in work all the time, double-checking everything I did as I went.

As time was fast-forwarded, it showed Emanii and King also succumbing to the same fates. They worked for someone else and became miserable, just how I appeared. While it didn't seem to be any issues with money, we were each missing the most important thing in a home, love. Time was rarely spent with each other and all time seemed to be directed towards working long hours.

There was no laughing and going on adventures, like I had been shown at the previous house. Rather, they were spent working to get good grades or successes that ultimately led to unhappiness at all ends. There was less laughing, more work, and less meaningful results because of it. Everything in that version of my life resembled death and decay.

We magically teleported back to the lake where I was sent after my accident. However, I was teleported back to the lake alone. The little girl was not there, and neither was my grandmother. I went over to the lake where the little girl and I once sat, and put my feet into the lake.

Upon placing my feet in the lake, clarity came rushing into me all at once. What the little girl was showing me was that I needed to make a choice. I could continue down the path I was currently on or I could take another path - one that was new to me and had never been ventured before. This new venture would ultimately bring different results, happier results, results I knew the consequences of beforehand.

*****

I woke up the next morning, walked out to the kitchen, and saw Jenayah coming out of the bathroom.

"Good morning, how are you doing this morning? Are you doing okay?" She turned to me and asked.

"Good morning," I responded. "I'm good. I just woke up from a good dream and have a great feeling about today."

"Oh yeah, why is that?" Jenayah looked confused.

"I had a dream last night and was shown my future," I said.

As I continued explaining what my dream had shown to me, Emanii came out of her room and mentioned that she had a similar dream to mine last night.

In puzzlement, Jenayah and I both said, "What was your dream about?"

"Well, I am not sure anymore. I cannot remember everything about the dream. I just remember seeing a not-so-distant life where we lived by the water and seemed to be happy."

While in the physical, this was a thirteen-year-old girl standing in front of me talking at this moment; this was an old, ancient soul within. She was incredibly wise, beyond her time. She always captivated me in conversation every time we talked about the infinite possibilities of the future and where we saw ourselves going.

Jenayah and I both stood there in silence and astonishment at what we had just heard. It was almost as if I had received an instant and automatic confirmation from the universe, confirming what I dreamed was not just a dream. It was confirming what I had seen would be made physical at some point soon. If I made the right choice(s) along the way.

"I must get ready to take off and catch my plane back home. I need to leave here in thirty minutes. Are you going to be okay here alone? Do you need me to get you anything before I go?" Jenayah asked, interrupting my thoughts.

"No, I am okay. You got us pretty stocked up over here. We are good for a month, maybe even two!"

Trying my best to smile, I was crying on the inside and was honestly afraid of being alone again. I looked over at Emanii and it was as if she could read my face. She came over to me and hugged me. We stood there for a couple of seconds before Jenayah joined in on the hugging action. It felt nice to be surrounded and wrapped in love, especially right now. King finally waking up, came out of his room.

"Good morning, everyone! I just had a weird dream," he said.

"Everybody is having dreams in this house BUT me," replied Jenayah bursting into laughter.

"What was the dream about?" I asked.

"I don't really know... But we were all very sad."

He suddenly fell quiet and I could tell he did not want to go any further. King is another old soul. He is a nine-year-old boy with the wisdom of an eighty-year-old man. When he would speak, it would be of few words, but every word spoken had deep significance. He put thought into his word selection and took time to handpick his words before speaking them, like how I picked out my work clothes for the next day. I admired this attribute about him and often wish I had this attribute myself.

"Well, the good news is that it was just a dream," I replied. "It's up to the interpreting dreamer to determine whether the dream is good or bad. But I feel it is also important to remember that there is no good or bad; there is only our interpretation of these things and circumstances, that can make them good or bad. If you always try to find the good, you usually get that right back. If you always try to find the bad, you will get that back too."

King came over and hugged me tightly. I could feel his relief as he put his head on my chest.

"I love you, Mommy," King said.

"I love you more," I replied.

"Okay, it's time for me to head out," said Jenayah. "Cam, I'll call you once I get to the airport, so you know I made it."

We all gave our kisses and hugs goodbye to Jenayah. We made some breakfast and sat down to eat. I could only eat so much before the nausea became unbearable from the pain of my injuries. I took a pain pill, laid down on the couch, and drifted off to sleep. This time when I drifted to sleep, it took me back to the hospital bed where I previously was. The little girl suddenly appeared in the background.

"Remember this woman?" She asked.

"Yes," I replied.

"What's the difference between the woman in the bed and the woman on the couch right now?"

I looked over at myself lying in the hospital bed, then turned around to see myself asleep on the couch. Both versions were under heavy sedation from the narcotics given to me by the hospital. I was in so much pain that I was nauseated and unable to function properly. I was never usually one to give in to the pain and take medication for it.

This was a completely different circumstance. I was just thrown out of a truck for goodness' sake! The little girl then said, "Remember, you are not a prisoner, nor are you a victim. You are a lot stronger than you think. Incredible healing powers lay dormant inside of you. However, your nonbelief in its existence is what is delaying your healing.

"You do not need the medication you are taking; it will keep you from the truth you seek. It is time you stand and face your pain and the reality of it. Along with the things that brought you here. By doing this, you will be freed and what you seek, will be delivered."

"What do you mean by freed?" I asked a bit confused.

"You can only understand from your current level of perception. Do not focus your energy on the things of the past. Instead, focus all your energy on creating what is to be. What you are meant to know will make its way to you, at the right time."

Just like that, the little girl disappeared in a white, smoke-like vapor. A few hours later when I woke up, I checked my phone and noticed a missed call with a text from Jenayah letting me know she made it back home safely and to call her back later. I went into my bathroom and looked opened my medicine cabinet, knowing what I had to do.

I grabbed the pain pills and opened the bottle, pouring the entire stock into the toilet. *Hopefully, I don't regret this later,* I thought to myself. As I turned around, Emanii was standing with eyes as big as saucers.

"What have you done?!" Screamed Emanii.

"Calm down. I will be fine. It is something I must do." I responded calmly. I did not want her to worry.

"Mom, they gave you those pills for a reason. You just took flight out of the window of your truck a couple of days ago. You should have asked the doctor first."

"I understand you feel worried, 'Manii, but you should not. I am doing what I feel is best. These pills make it hard for me to know whether I am healing. If I keep numbing the pain, how will I ever know if I am getting better? I also do not need a weak leg because I am lying around all the time, asleep, due to these pain meds. Sometimes, you must put pain on pain to heal."

"I get it, but I think you should have at least left a few for yourself... You know, for those painful days."

"I will be okay. I am stronger than you think."

I smiled and took her hand, pulling her closer to me. I hugged her tightly, and told her again not to worry. The next few days were the hardest. The pain radiated throughout my entire body. I did not have an appetite, and my body was weak from lack of nourishment. All I could think about was the pain and nothing more.

When I would fall asleep, I would sleep for short stints of time, unable to dream. When I would wake up, I would be completely drenched in a cold sweat. This lasted for almost a week until I woke up one morning and decided I had enough. I realized if I did not eat, sleep, and hydrate thoroughly, I would never heal.

There was a clear choice I had to make. I could either call my doctor, tell him what I had done and see if more pain meds could be called in. Or, I could stand and face my pain; tapping into the healing powers that were inside of me. I got up and took a nice, hot shower. The water felt refreshing - as if a new person was being born.

I got out and put my lotion on, spraying a little of my favorite body spray. I threw some clothes on, then headed to the kitchen, where I planned to make a wonderful breakfast feast! As I headed toward the kitchen area, I could smell something already cooking. Emanii was standing in the kitchen doing something by the sink. I walked over to her and noticed she was whipping pancake batter together in a bowl.

"What are you doing up so early?" I asked her.

"You have not been feeling well and you also have not been eating anything. So, I wanted to make you something nice to wake up to. It was supposed to be a surprise." Emanii replied.

"You are such a sweetheart, but I got this. Besides, it is kind of like my job and all to cook for you and your brother."

"It's okay to receive help, Mommy. We all need it sometimes."

"Thank you, my baby. I am so blessed to have such an amazing daughter like you. You and your brother make my life worth living! Can I join you in making breakfast?"

This absolutely broke my heart! My daughter should not be taking care of me right now. It should be the other way around! I was so mad at myself but refused to break down and cry like so many nights before.

"I do not think you should stand on that leg right now. Seriously, you should lie down to let your eye and leg heal, Mommy. This is something I can do. I have watched you many times." Emanii appeared very concerned at this point.

"I promise, I am fine. If I keep babying myself, I will never heal. Since the accident, I have had plenty of sleep and I do not need any more of it."

She handed me the pancake batter and began preparing the kitchen table for breakfast. I finished up making breakfast and then went in King's room to wake him up. We had a beautiful breakfast together as a family, and with me as a new mother. It was time to heal from the inside out. I committed myself to see this through, promising to never give up, no matter what it took.

To jump start the much-needed healing, I started taking long, brisk walks, going up and then back down the stairs to my apartment. Putting more pain on the current pain. Being in pain taught me a lot of things, but what I liked most is the fact that the pain kept me from my thoughts. The physical training was excruciating in the beginning but as time progressed, it became easier and less painful.

I wanted to get back to normal and resume my life. More than anything, I wanted this chapter of my life to be closed along with the pain and psychological damage caused. I figured the sooner things go back to normal, the better everything would be. I decided it was time to go back to work, even though I was not even remotely close to being fully healed.

It had only been two weeks since my accident, but I wanted things to go back to normal as soon as possible. Preparing for my return to work, I ordered a new, black BMW X5 with a few additional safety features. The truck was delivered to my home three days later, which marked my return to work the following day.

I pulled up to the office building and put my shades on to hide my black eyes and eyelid stitches. *Thank goodness for hair,* I thought to myself. The swoop bang I made completely hid the lump on the top of my forehead that was still protruding profusely. The limp from my broken leg could not be hidden, but most of the people I worked with were aware of the horrible car accident I was involved in. So, a limp, at the least, should be expected.

I entered the office and slowly went up the stairs to the second floor, where my desk was located. The moment I got up the stairs and opened the door, everyone immediately ran over to me asking how I was doing and letting me know I was in their prayers. I entertained some conversations, but I just wanted to go back to work. I hated being treated like a victim. I sat down at my desk and opened my briefcase, pulling out my laptop to begin my day.

While waiting for my computer to boot up, I looked around the office and noticed everyone looked miserable and depressed. No one was smiling or laughing, and now that the excitement from my return had dissipated, it was also eerily quiet. Although I was used to this, being a mortgage underwriter, it still struck me as odd and took me back to the visions of my dream with the two versions of myself.

For lunch, I decided I would leave and go home. I did not want to go to lunch with anyone and wanted time to myself to sort through my thoughts. I made a peanut butter and jelly sandwich and went out to my balcony. I sat down taking in the beautiful smells and sights, as if for the first time. On my drive back to the office, it suddenly hit me like a ten-pound bag of potatoes!

The way I was currently living was the second house the little girl brought me to. It is like I could see how everything would play out if I chose to stay within the confines of all I knew. I became determined and eager for change. I could not do the same things and go on believing I would get different results. I started thinking about my life, my future, and the changes I needed to make to bring them together.

After work, I came back home. Seven pages of notes and several hours later, I had reached my exhaustion point. After cooking dinner and putting the kids to bed, I crawled into my bed. I picked up my notes, read them, and made additional notes until I fell asleep.

*****

Entering this dream state, I was met by the little girl, at the lake. She was sitting at the lake with her feet in the water. I walked toward her and sat down next to her, also placing my feet in the water.

"You are finally seeing the truth, Camryn. I'm proud of you. You are headed in the right direction and your next steps will be the hardest. You are and always have been extremely blessed, guided, and protected by a higher power. This will never change.

"You must trust yourself and the abilities you have been given; this is your internal compass, placed in you at creation. Remember that in the days ahead, and also remember that doubt cancels faith, and faith cancels doubt."

As the little girl disappeared, I was teleported back to the first house the little girl showed me in my dream before. I could not only see myself this time, but I could feel everything she was feeling, as if we were one. This journey merged the experiences of the observer and the observed into one and, at that moment, I was this first version of myself.

I could operate this vessel as if I was living in this new life, eventually becoming unaware that we were two different people. There was always an abundance of love, safety, and protection that was surrounding me all the time in a way I had never experienced before. I did not want these feelings to ever end!

*****

I woke up to the beautiful sun on my face, but as I looked around, it looked nothing like the place I just was at. Realizing the experience was a dream, I was brought back to a bitter reality. It angered me, being taken into one reality to be dropped off in another! It created mass confusion, but once the anger passed, it created the motivation I needed to take the next steps.

I could not continue living the life I was living any longer. I felt like a fraud; this life did not belong to me, nor did it represent me, or who I am now. Things had to change, and so I decided it was time to take a break. I deleted all my social media accounts, deleted most of my contacts, and started envisioning this new life of mine. This is a new Cam, with a new life, and I can recreate myself however I choose!

~ 3 ~

CHAPTER THREE:

ALCHEMY

They saying goes that the grass is not greener on the other side,
but I have never agreed nor understood that statement. The grass
is always greener where it is cared for and watered properly.

We work the same way as every other living organism – light
being the bearer or shape and life; death being the bearer of death
and transformation.

Reality stands in the middle as a test of our landscape; holding a
testament to the fruits of our labors.

I lay in bed awake at night, only half asleep. The moment I doze off, I get a sudden flash of crashing into the tree and everything going black. I am then jolted back into being awake where I lay with my eyes wide open; deep in thought. I turn the TV on to find something comforting to watch and then begin that same process repeatedly.

Sleep is no longer a realistic thing to me; it is becoming a distant memory, a figment of my imagination. It is becoming hard to tell the difference between dreams and reality anymore, they are all running together into one big loop. Life is happening so fast, that I cannot make sense of anything.

Months are becoming weeks, weeks are becoming days, and days are becoming hours. I receive calls and text messages that go unanswered for several days, and sometimes, weeks. My voicemail has become so full, it no accepts new messages. I did not want to talk to anyone, and I did not want to see anyone. I just wanted to be left alone. Left alone to decipher what all this meant and what I was supposed to do with it.

I so desperately wanted a visit from the little girl to gain additional clarity. I had not seen her in a dream for several months. I felt hopeless, abandoned, and worst of all, I felt lost, all over again. While my mental acuity was rather off, my body was getting stronger with the pain becoming less noticeable.

My body's muscle definition became much more defined, with noticeable transformations taking place - both physically and mentally. My detached personality took over my personal and professional life. The only lasting attachments I felt were to my children.

I was no longer concerned with understanding the people and circumstances of my past and present.

I was solely focused on creating the future self that was shown to me in my dream months ago. Changes to my mindset and perception took the biggest toll, leaving me with the conclusion that change was necessary for my evolvement. It was time to move and get a change of scenery. I decided Florida would be where I would begin my new life, and create a new me.

A couple of months later, I purchased a four-bedroom home with a pool on an island in northern Florida. I got it for a bargain right before the property value surge in 2021. It was my first home, and I was proud to be a first-time homeowner. I looked at my current disposition and felt truly happy for the first time in a very long time. I could not believe how far I had come and the progress I was making.

When life happens, it is easy for the most major moments of our lives to be swept away in the daily happenings of life. I decided to journal this moment along with my other accomplishments, so I would never forget the feeling of accomplishment on this day. I began my journal entry with:

Since the accident, I have moved to Florida. I purchased my first home, and made a cushy six-figure salary. Both of my kids are taking honor courses at school, with all our health being impeccable and in perfect condition. I had so much to be thankful for and began looking back at where I was just last year.

I was renting an apartment and partying every weekend. I made less money and had nothing but a bunch of empty relationships everywhere I went. There was no investment in anything long-term, and there was no investment being put into myself. I treated everything as a momentary pleasure; nothing ever mattered.

I was able to walk away from anything and anyone with a moment's notice, and that is how I preferred it. Now, I had put down roots and was becoming the exact opposite of everything I once was. Everything I had previously all reflected short-term thinking; thinking of a true survivalist. The thinking of my mother, who was also a single mother. She met my father when she was stationed in Frankfort, Germany, while both were serving in the Army.

They were new enlistments who had freshly joined, both coming from severely broken homes, with severely damaged parents. The thing about broken people is that they go around breaking other people - creating more just like them. My mother came from a family who was white and predominately racist.

They did not take her choosing to be with a black man very well. They decided to serve her disownment papers while she was in Germany. Every family member signed that vile doc except three brave souls. My great grandparents being two of those brave souls.

My grandparents were fresh off the boat that entered Ellis Island, New York, in 1920 from Austria. I believe they understood somewhat the hardships of being a minority in America, as to why they never stood by my family's hurtful and evil ways. My father's family were deep-rooted southern folk. My grandfather was killed when my dad was five years old.

Leaving my grandmother Lena alone to raise him, along with his younger sister and older brother on her own. My grandma Lena was something fierce from what I am told, she was an Eastern Star who practiced voodoo and black magic. She always scared me a little, and I think she scared my father too.

He moved to Connecticut when he was twelve and was raised by his uncle. My father would never speak about his family. He never told us family stories and was never willing to be open about them either. He was closed off and took his pain out on us frequently, my mother taking the brunt of it.

With both parents coming from broken homes, abuse was a common practice. My father would hit my mother and choke her up against the wall where her feet would just dangle from the floor. This would happen right in front of me and my brothers, for little to no reason at all. This would go on for several hours all of the time.

He would even choke her in public, right in front of strangers and nothing was ever done. I never understood why my mother kept going back to take more, but it was almost as if she was addicted to the abuse he was routinely administered. This sick cycle went on for almost twenty years before she had finally had enough.

He took everything from her, most of which she would never get back, including herself. I can remember one time when my mom was pregnant and they had gotten into another one of their knock-down, drag-out fights. I was crying in the corner, so worried about her belly and him hurting my brother that was inside.

They only had one car at that time, so after he was done with his usual rant, he took off with the car and left my mom and I home alone. This was disastrous as the fight sent my mother into labor with no car to take her to the hospital. With no car and no one to call, she put my coat on me and walked herself to the nearest hospital.

There were about twelve to fourteen inches of snow on the ground at the time, and I can remember my mother dragging me through all that snow as she was going into labor. Due to my size, I could barely keep up with the snow being about as tall and high as I was. I saw red drops of blood going into the snow as she drugs us through, but I knew better than to say anything and feared what I knew to be true.

That night was the death of her son, and my brother. However, that death began the birth of a new beginning, rekindling her relationship with her family. This was the first time she saw her grandparents in years. They came up to get her after she lost my brother, and we stayed with them until she could get on her feet and get away from my father.

Although they helped her to get away from him, numerous times, she would always go right back. She never learned anything from all the times before. She never seemed to care much about the countless infidelities or ongoing abuse. He was always over at our house all the time, creating the same abusive chaos, every time.

Over eight years since losing her first son, she then proceeded to give him two more sons. Then, one beautiful day, I guess she finally had enough and filed for divorce. I thought divorcing him would have been the best thing for her, but it turned out to be even more detrimental than the constant physical, verbal, and emotional abuse.

Divorcing him figuratively killed my mother. She mentally checked out shortly thereafter and was never the same since. My mom worked making minimum wage, supporting herself and three children with little to no help from my father. My father cared very little about us, unless it involved us getting into trouble at school.

My mother would frequently use that as an excuse to call him over to the house, which always resulted in extreme beatings with belts that left us bruised all over our bodies. We never had much of anything but each other. Knowing this, I always made sure my brothers showered before school and had clean clothes to put on.

I would check their homework for them, talked to them about how their days were going, and most importantly, did what I could to keep them out of trouble. If we had any food in the house, I would try to pack a lunch for them to take. However, most days we had absolutely nothing in the house, other than tap water. We would survive on a pack of bologna, a loaf of bread, a carton of eggs, and a bag of potatoes every week, usually leaving nothing to eat by about Thursday.

My brothers and I qualified for reduced lunch at school, but seldomly ate because we did not even have the thirty-five cents we needed for the reduced rate. Especially when that reduced rate increased to fifty cents. This would require my mother to give us one dollar and fifty cents a day, for all three of us. And, she never seemed to have lunch money for us, ever.

We could never go on field trips because we never had the fees required to be able to go. Resulting in us missing out on a lot of the experiences all the other students got to be a part of. Sports were also out of the question because of the money. Thus, creating an atmosphere for us to be isolated and bullied at school.

We were bullied constantly about the holes in our shoes and the continuous repeat of clothing we had to wear. Having only two to three shirts, one good pair of pants, and one or two sweatshirts; all of which were passed down to us from family members who could no longer fit them. We never got new clothes, new shoes, or anything nice at all.

As time progressed and her mental check-out got gradually worse, she went from doing hardly anything at all to doing nothing at all. She showered maybe once a week and was over four hundred pounds. Our home was often filthy and smelly. My mother hardly ever cleaned anything in the house or did any laundry, so the piles of clothes and filth would accumulate and turn into infestations of roaches and rats everywhere.

No matter how much I would clean, the mess would be right back within a day or two, as if I had cleaned nothing at all. By the time I was fifteen, I got a job and started giving my money to my mother to help with the food and the utility bills. However, even though I pitched in money to help things out around the house, we would still have our electricity shut off and had no groceries.

At sixteen, I decided to enter a program at high school that would allow me to work a full-time job and leave school a bit early to do so; all while getting the high school credits I needed to graduate. Thinking that more money from my now full-time hours plus her income would surely help, I continued giving my money to my mother.

Yet and still, we never had any groceries and still had our utilities shut off. By the time I was seventeen, I had enough of the nonsense and told my mother I was moving out. My friend Jenayah and I got an apartment together and split the expenses equally, both working at the same place, and it worked out perfectly...until it didn't. Jenayah started becoming almost unbearable to be around.

She started becoming jealous of everything I had, including my friends and my relationship. This resulted in years of turmoil and endless chaos and drama. I felt like my life had become like the movie "The Roommate," but in real life. She stalked all my friends, my boyfriend, and even me; blaming it on "good intentions" and "trying to look out for me."

These shenanigans got old after some time, forcing me to get my own place. Even after getting my own place, she still would not leave me alone and would track me down everywhere I went. It truly became something out of a horror story, I could not get rid of her! She would always force herself on people and made everyone feel hella uncomfortable. I guess I kind of felt sorry for her and over time, allowed her back into my life. This decision always came with much regret.

At nineteen, my high school boyfriend and I found out that I was pregnant with Emanii and by twenty-three, I was pregnant with King. The unfortunate thing about most high school sweethearts is that they get to see the good with the bad, while they are growing up and still maturing. If they are lucky, they grow together and become stronger but oftentimes, they grow apart.

Again, the most unfortunate thing about broken people is that they tend to attract other broken people and continue the same cycles of chaos. I did not fall far from my mother's steps. I then spent the next sixteen years dealing with the very same verbal, emotional, and at times physical abuse.

Unable to take anymore, one night while he was at work, I packed up as much of our things as I could and I got me and my children out to safety. I moved us into a new place and I filed for divorce the following day. After the divorce, I found a lot of new freedom I had never experienced before and met a lot of different people.

I learned a lot about myself and others, but most importantly, I learned the value of myself. I may never understand why I had to go through some things that I did, but what I understand is that it all went into who I am today. My track history proved I was a survivalist, but today I choose to be different, think different, and see different from that of a survivalist.

I choose to be a strategist; realizing who I am today is constantly changing and evolving. Who I am today is not who I will be a month from now or even a year from now. I no longer questioned things about my past, who I am, or the reasons and purpose of the accident. Everything happened for a reason. The reason(s) given within their due season. I felt free and safe for the first time in my entire life and it felt amazing!

This feeling of safety is something I have never experienced before and as I ended my journal entry; I knew I was entering a new phase in my life. I was being leveled up to something greater and could feel it in my bones. That night when I went to bed, I felt something happening inside of me.

It was igniting a yearning, a burning desire to do something greater with my life. Even though I was finally safe and content with where I was, something in me was telling me it was time for more change. I did not know where this feeling came from, but it was all I could think about as I fell asleep.

I wanted and needed more to feel alive. This need and want were not for anything of material possessions and substance, but for something that provided a deeper meaning and purpose to life itself.

*****

As I drifted off to sleep, I suddenly arrived at the lake. The little girl sitting on the wooden swing, swinging back and forth. Her curls glistened from the rays of the sun, being gently whisked around by the flowing air.

"Did you miss me?" The little girl asked.

"I missed you a lot. I was not sure if I was ever going to see you again," I responded.

"Have you ever heard of alchemy?" She asked, going higher and higher in the swing.

"The Alchemist is one of my favorite books," I replied with a giggle.

"I knew you were going to say that. Isn't it kind of funny how the truth always surrounds us, even when we don't know it's there?"

"What do you mean?"

"Consider the very definition of alchemy, which is like a super-power or some kind of special process(s) that can transmute one thing into another, in very mysterious ways. You always wanted to be an alchemist, and now you are the ultimate alchemist. Don't you think?"

As I stood there in silence, I realized what she was saying and just smiled in response.

"I want to show you something. Will you come with me?" She stopped swinging back and forth on the swing, preparing to leap off it.

"Of course," I replied.

She hopped off the swing, and we headed over to the lake. She sat down beside the lake, across from the usual spot we sat. She grabbed my hand and pulled me into the lake with her. Fully submerged in the water she turned around and faced me.

"Let go and trust the process," she said.

As I let go and relaxed my body, we both began to drop through an opening portal underwater. As we descended into the portal, it was as if time completely froze. We were suspended there, and I felt weightless. I closed my eyes, terrified by what I was seeing.

"Open your eyes and breathe," she whispered.

I could hear a voice interrupting my thoughts. I opened my eyes and took a breath. I could not believe what I was seeing. This was the first time she revealed herself to me.

"You look exactly like me, the younger me. My family use to call me Pooh. You remind me of myself in my family photos."

"I am you; your purest form. I was unable to face you until you faced yourself. Always remember, as above, so below."

Just then, we were sent to a place that was so bright, it hurt to keep my eyes open. I closed them and kept slowly blinking until I could fully open them. Once I could keep my eyes open, I began to look around in shock and awe of what I was seeing.

"What is this place?" I asked.

It looked like we were standing on something soft and pure white, like snow. We remained weightless as we floated toward the sun.

"Go over to the edge and look down," Pooh said to me.

I walked over to the edge of where I was standing and looked down.

"WHOA!" I exclaimed!

I could not believe my eyes. The white, soft thing we were standing on was a cloud. This cloud was floating so high in the air it made everything look like little ants below. It was an odd feeling because while I was immediately struck with my normal extreme fear of heights, the fear dissipated as quickly as it came in. I felt unusually safe, at peace, and in total comfort.

The only thing I could feel was the anticipation of where this cloud was taking us. As we continued moving toward the sun, I noticed I could feel that same warmth again, similarly to the night of my accident. It was a blissful feeling and I could feel it pulling me in, like a magnet. I looked down over the cloud again and the earth was below our feet.

However, instead of there being only one Earth, there were multiple piles of the Earth below, infinite in fact. They just kept going. The Earth's below resembled dome-shaped objects placed around a flat surface of the Earth, giving off the appearance that it was round like a complete circle. As we floated upward in space, nearing the sun, we entered the abyss. It was completely dark and I could no longer see anything at all.

Yet and still, even amid complete darkness, I did not feel alone. I knew I was being protected and guided by a higher power throughout this journey wherever we were going. As we moved effortlessly and rapidly through this dark space, my body became a stronger magnet. While I was being pulled towards the sun, I was being filled with complete sense of total euphoria.

Suddenly, I noticed a circle directly in the middle of the sun opening in a swirling manner. The swirling manner created enough force to pull us directly into the center of the circle, which then became another portal. This portal was filled with brightness everywhere. But, this time it didn't hurt my eyes to look at this magnificent spectacle before me.

I could see a dark dot coming into view. As we approached this dark dot, I felt a cooling sensation take over me. The cloud we were originally riding on was no longer beneath our feet. I could see everything directly below, above, and to the sides. In an instant, some kind of mysterious watery substance came swirling about creating a smoke-like vapor.

The air all around us became filled with noises and voices coming from the vapors. The vapors turned into smoke and catapulted us into the brightest of light where two pillars emerged.

"We have arrived. We will be there shortly," said Pooh.

As we entered this beautiful place, the first thing I noticed was the gold that was everywhere. It created a shimmering effect that echoed all over the land. There were tall, buildings, statues, and cars made of pure gold. There were yellow, green, blue, red, and purple lights glittering and sparkling everywhere, radiating off the gold fixtures.

The water was crystal-clear, cerulean blue, with a tinge of a green Caribbean color around the inner parts of the water. The sand was pure white with blues and greens that folded into it. Tall, leafy trees surrounded the edges of the water. We made our descent close to a tall white-gold castle that had blue, mirror-like windows.

The castle was nestled on the sand right by the water that was surrounded by rich forestry. There were white, green, and gold flags with a symbol I was unfamiliar with. The symbol was a square with the four elements of air, fire, water, and earth at the corners. Inside of the square had the symbol of a cross with an infinity ribbon going around it. The cross had two pairs of wings that attached to it.

There was a circle in the middle of the cross that had a gold phoenix, wolf looking thing in the center of it. The roof of the castle had a royal purple light that emanated above it. The symbol was also fixed in the center of the rooftop in gold and white trim around the edge, encased in a circle. We landed directly in the middle of this circle.

When my feet touched the plates to the gold symbol, the gold started to make its way up my body like some kind of liquid armor, clinging to my body like a glove. It began covering my feet, going up my legs, over my stomach, arms, and fingers, and finally up to my neck, where it halted. The liquid armor started moving around on my chest and a white gold emblem of that same symbol atop the roof appeared. Chest and shoulder plates formed of this same white gold with the number seven becoming engraved within the chest plate.

I looked over and Pooh's transformation mirrored that of my own. The circle we landed on began opening from the middle and we descended into the castle. As the circle closed above us, a gold crown was lowered upon our heads. As we were making our way down this mirrored tunnel, I could see myself through the reflections.

These reflections were bringing memories back to me, but none of them were clear, they were bits and fragments of distant memories. I knew I was in a familiar place, but I could not quite put together where exactly I knew this place from. Instantly it hit me, I was *home*. Pooh then turned to me.

"Remember who you are," she said.

As she said this, I found myself alone, back in the abyss again. I closed my eyes and could feel I was moving extremely fast, unsure where I was going. I opened my eyes, and I suddenly stopped moving. I became suspended, floating in this space when I felt a surge of lightning jolt through my entire body.

With the surge of each volt, which became a fury of flames; I received a memory, and each memory contained a branch of other memories. I could suddenly remember other lives I had lived before this one. Many of them, spanning millions of years. I remembered many wars I fought and won, single-handedly. I created millions of children that are still creating children to this very day. I have lived many lives and recreated myself within each one every single time.

When the surge of information stopped, I reeled it all in. Taking in every detail, analyzing each piece of information given, but found there were many missing components. I could not move but felt my physical form had transformed, once again, during the surge of flames. A white portal opened above me and my body began elevating towards the portal.

Upon first entering the portal, I felt another jolt of energy hit my body like a surge of lightning. As the energy made its way up my body, it stopped about halfway up my back - which began splitting apart. With beams of lightning surging into all directions of my body, a pair of wings emerged, as if they had been there all along, but now they were finally free.

The surge of energy continued making its way up into my head and then ran back down my new body through my legs. I was now fully transformed into my original nature as the phoenix wolf. As I made my way through the portal, now with even greater speed, more of my memories came flooding in, adding to the greatness of the flames and speed.

I was growing bigger by the moment. The more I remembered, the more the flame grew that was purely controlled by the rage growing inside of me. I departed the portal and flew right into the Holy Place with a crash!

"You must control the rage. Remember who you are, please. Remember who you are," pleaded Pooh who came running out of the sanctuary towards me.

"This is not you and you can't see everything right now. You must control your rage, please, I can help you remember if you take my hand. You are blinded with rage; you must control it and resist the rage! Please trust me and take my hand."

As Pooh slowly made her way toward me, she approached me looking me directly in my eyes, putting out her hand.

"You have to take my hand for this to work," she said.

Trusting her, I placed my hand in hers and could feel the rage dissipate almost immediately. As the rage went away, I transformed back into the liquid gold glove covering, this time with my wings still intact. We entered the sanctuary and the tall candles on the gold pillars lit up, lighting the way as we made our way down the hall.

As we approached the end of the hall, a pair of doors appeared out of nowhere, opening for us to enter. I made my way down the aisle, taking in the throne that floated amongst the white clouds above, below, and all around us. There were tall, gold pillars everywhere with candles attached to them. They had gold artwork etched all over them.

Above the seat of each chair were names etched in gold with corresponding animals, numbers, and associated ruling planet names.

"Please take your seat, we have a lot to cover," Pooh said.

Without hesitation, as if acting from a prior memory, I took my seat at Minerva, number seven.

"As a child, you were always strategically placed in an environment that would cultivate your growth. This environment gave you the experiences, tools, and resources needed to become who you are now. The pain was a requirement for your specific evolvement, ultimately changing and shaping the course of your entire journey.

"The love and lack thereof were necessary components, for within the absence, grew a presence. That presence, who was there all along, made you who you are now and who you will become later. As above, so below, and as below, so above. It is important to know and always remember that nothing can operate outside of those bounds," Pooh continued.

"The Indygos are the enlightened ones that are the celestial warriors working through reciprocal relationships. These relationships were established before you were created. The Indygos are the messengers, protectors, and warriors who keep balance in check.

"When things become out of balance, at certain designated times, that is when the Indygos are activated and prepared for the things to come. At conception, God's DNA was strategically configured into Indygo's DNA, making the connection between Indygo and God complete.

"Similar to the work of a magician pulling a rabbit out of an empty hat; you are known as the master alchemist above and below, because only you can directly connect to the higher power. You employ a collective insight and strategy needed for things to come ahead. You are a goddess of many things; wisdom and war being two of them.

"Every thirty-six hundred years, we make our way through the sun portal to reset life. This resets all energies; where they are taken in, blended, and placed to establish the next thirty-six hundred years of evolvement. Darkness and light are not filtered and ignorance cannot divide the two. Thus, requiring the filtration process to become manual, ensuring balance is kept and ignorance is swept away with the truth, the way, and the light.

"The filtration process is manual but inscribed within creation itself. Each birth of evolution has a perfect time for balance to return. It written a very long time ago. Your resurrection was needed to activate a sequence of events that later assimilates into one of the biggest battles of all time. Your bloodshed from your accident was a divine sacrifice needed for you to harness the energy within and bring it into your world for the journey ahead.

"Keep in mind, as a mortal, both energies are housed within you, making it imperative that you always and only feed the right energy. You must learn to harness and balance these powers and abilities coming from both sides. If you do not find control over both energies, one of the two will find control over you.

"Three evils are lurking in plain sight yet remain hidden to the untrained eye. They want to control the power protected and hidden away within you, killing all mankind. You are the mother of all Indygos; breathing life into each of your creations and inscriptions. This power cannot be taken from you; however, it can be harnessed through you and leveraged by another, if you allow it.

"You must use *your* form of alchemy to channel the truth. Be careful in channeling the truth you seek, for there are many channels connected to the truth that all tell lies. It is up to you, the chosen one, to use discernment in choosing which channel is truth itself.

"Once the truth itself is channeled, you must seek additional information about the three evils, along with information and insight on what is to come. You must prepare for the battles ahead and create a balance for the rebirth ahead. As you make your way back to your shadow self, please remember who you are and never forget it!

"In forgetting who you are, you are forgetting your duties to mankind, which will cause the mass extinction of mankind altogether. It will leave no trace of balance or life of any kind. There will only be darkness, death, decay, chaos, and destruction. Channel the truth itself and let this truth guide your way."

*****

~ 4 ~

CHAPTER FOUR:

Seek and Ye Shall Find

Be careful looking into the abyss; for when you look into the abyss, abyss looks back into you.

I was not getting much sleep and my attention to detail with my job was slipping. I was gaining traction and focus in certain areas of my life but was losing it all at the same time in other areas. It was extremely difficult to see the importance of anything outside of what I was shown in my dream.

After many endless sleepless nights, I started making the most of them. I decided if I could not sleep, I would learn all that I could meanwhile. I started learning from a new perspective, seeing everything differently now, clearer, and without the static that was previously there. I could read with lightning speed, retaining all the new information with complete accuracy.

I was reading ten new books a week, and this did not include the magazines and online content. Once I had enough information, I started journaling and tracking commonalities I found amongst the writings. My results after the first month were astounding. There were quite a few commonalities amongst the data I found, all linking to three major components.

All the endpoints pointed to the same three components that I discovered before. I decided I needed to take some time off work to get my head together and figure out my next steps. I began researching online for vacation rental homes available that would provide the resources and amenities I need to channel the truth.

I found an excellent five-bedroom estate near Big Pine Key, Florida that came with its own private island and boat to use during my accommodation. Seeming like the perfect solution for my problem at hand, I booked immediately. We pulled up to the lavish estate booked for our stay for the next couple of days. This was such a sight for sore eyes, especially after a seven-and-a-half-hour road trip coming down from Jacksonville.

"This is what's up!" exclaimed King.

"I know, right!!" yelled Emanii. "Thank you, Mom! This is the best trip ever! Can we take that boat over there out today?!"

"I need to get some rest before I do anything. I am thinking it will be tomorrow before I am ready to go anywhere. Once I put my things away, I will order some food and have it delivered. Go ahead and find your rooms and get your things put away."

"Okay, we will." Both kids replied, racing to their preferred room of choice.

I headed to the master bedroom and put away my things. I opened the windows and balcony room door, then ordered some pizza. I was so exhausted and needed to sleep severely. Once the pizza came, I took a hot shower and laid down in bed. I was more than ready to sleep and my body welcomed it this time.

I could not remember the last time I had a decent night of sleep or any kind of sleep lasting over two to three hours at a time, since my dream. The sound of the waves crashing on the ocean shore put me right to sleep within moments of my head touching the pillow. I somehow slept through to the next day.

When I woke up, I looked over at the balcony doors and noticed someone had closed them. I grabbed my gray robe I left hanging on the edge of the bed and made my way to check out the rest of the house. The house was immaculate, with no dishes in sight, nothing lying around that needed to be picked up. Both kids were in their beds asleep.

Man, this is perfect, I thought to myself. I made my way around the house verifying nothing major happened while I was asleep. The kitchen was clean and pristine, shockingly. Through the kitchen window, I could see a white boat, with blue trim and writing along it bobbing in the dark water. I felt extremely blessed and very fortunate to be able to take in and have access to this beautiful scenery.

After making sure everything was copasetic, I headed back to my room and rolled up a fat doobie! I went out to the balcony area and got comfortable with my dear friend, Mary Jane. It had been years since me and my good friend MJ had spoken. We were more than overdue for a nice catch up!

I lit up and took a deep breath in and exhaled my stress away. Me being the lightweight that I am, a couple of puffs later, I put it out and sat back in the lounge chair. The enormous amount of clarity given from the negligible amount of weed smoked was highly invigorating.

I thought back to my dream and the things I was shown, still vividly remembering every detail. I started examining my current life in greater detail. I did not understand why I had a sudden change of heart about my current profession. No matter how hard I tried, I could not locate the source point for this sudden struggle. However, I knew I could only keep putting off attending to this matter for so long.

I used to like underwriting mortgages, the problem solving that comes with it, and the excellent money. But now I felt like it no longer represented who I am. I dreaded the thought of going back to work and knew I needed something more. I needed something that fell in line with what I believed my purpose here is. Something less daunting and less time consuming.

I knew I was on a timeline to get these things figured out, but that timeline did not apply to me at this moment. The only thing that mattered to me was spending time with my children and myself. I looked toward the sky at the pinkish hue caressing the shoreline in the distance. The sun rising reminded me of traveling through it, over to the other side.

It also made me wonder how and why time is so different from one state of being to another. When I dream, it is as if time completely stops or does not exist at all. The last dream I had, felt like weeks, maybe even months long. When I woke up from that dream, I had only been asleep for seven hours. I continued reminisced a little while longer, and then decided it was time to get the day started.

I wanted to take the boat out to the private island today and stay the night up there. I had only driven a boat a few times in life, but driving a boat of this size was a first. I went back inside, showered, and changed into my usual white t-shirt and jean shorts, then threw on my Sperry boat shoes to match.

I woke both kids up and went into the kitchen to start breakfast. I grabbed the potatoes, eggs, bacon, onion, bell pepper, and vegetable oil. Commencing to get to work making my most craved and talked about breakfast burritos! We needed something hearty to carry us throughout the day on our journey. We ate our breakfast, grabbed our things, and headed out to the boat.

"We are going to check out that private island today kiddos, so make sure you bring your electronics, an overnight bag, and a book. I plan to spend the night there. The cooler has water, sodas, and juices in it. Snacks and sandwiches are in the mini-fridge below the deck."

Emanii and King were the best little sidekicks! They were always down for an adventure, no matter what time it was. Dealing with a mother who does just about everything out of complete spontaneity has to be tedious, but they somehow take it in stride. True champs! Emanii's hair was flowing in the wind and glistened in the sun, as the boat caressed the surface of the water with great speed.

I then looked over to King, who was looking over the boat at the water smiling from ear to ear. He had this look in his eyes like this was one of the best moments of his life. We arrived at the island shortly thereafter and put away our things in the house on the island.

We spent most of the day watching dolphins, surfing, and exploring the different parts of the island on jet skis; until my hunger took over, no longer willing to be ignored. We headed back to the house on the island to get the charcoals ready for this evening's dinner. The kids, however, did not seem ready to settle in for the night.

"Hey Mom, can we go catch some waves?" King asked.

"Sure, just make sure you come back in about two hours. The food will be ready."

"What are you making?"

"Hotdogs, hamburgers, chicken wings, and steak with baked potatoes and broccoli."

"Ah, perfect! I love you, Mom!! You dabomb.com!" King still smiling ear to ear. His cute little dimples and beautiful smile could melt any girl's heart!

"We will not be gone long; we are just going to catch one wave and be right back. Love you, Mom!" Emanii said also smiling from ear to ear.

"I love you both more." One by one, Emanii and King bent down to give me a hug and a kiss before taking off with their surfboards. "Don't forget to put your leashes on this time, we don't need to lose more surfboards!"

"We won't," they both yelled back in unison.

After I got the grill together and had a nice flame going, I went back inside to prepare the meats I brought. I could not wait for this feast! There was nothing I loved more than a burger with a perfectly cooked, well-done porterhouse steak! Talk about a way to a girl's heart! I grabbed my phone and put on some music while getting things together.

Emanii and King returned sometime later, completely exhausted. It was written all over their faces. Things were going according to plan. I needed to be completely alone for the channeling to work I planned to do later that night. Once the process had begun, I could not allow for any disruptions.

"We caught like a thousand waves. You should have come, Mom. You would have loved it! I will be right back after I shower," Emanii said.

"Yeah Mom, it was dope! These waves are nothing like the ones we get where we live." King added.

"Maybe tomorrow we will go out and catch a few before we head back. We will go first thing in the morning. Sound good?" I asked.

"Sure does," said Emanii.

"Fo-sizzle," said King.

I went into the kitchen area and got their plates together. Once they returned from their showers, they ate their food, watched a little television, and were out like lights. A day full of sun will do that to ya! I woke them up and sent them to bed and headed back to my room.

I changed into the long, white, sheer dress from my bag that I brought with me. I grabbed my special red candle, a torch, my pocket knife, watch, and my black quilt blanket. I then headed out to the shoreline. I placed the blanket on the sand and took a seat. I began relaxing my mind until I had reached the quiet place where all things come to be.

I waited in the quiet place until I heard my watch beep, letting me know it was midnight. I headed over to the ocean and looked up at the blood moon. I entered the cool, dark water, planting my feet on the bottom sand firmly. I then made a diagonal cut in the palm of my left hand, drawing blood.

Raising my palm to the moon, the blood started running down my arm and onto my chest. I began chanting aloud, evoking the spirit of the truth itself. As the last words left my lips, "I invoke thee," everything went black instantaneously. I was no longer at the beach; I was taken elsewhere, into a place of pure abyss.

I could only see what was directly in front of me, thanks to the flame from the candle I brought. I could hear faint whispers in the background but I could not make out what they were saying. I held up my candle to give me a better glimpse into where I was at. I was in a cave and there was a long hallway of doors, in front of me.

Each door having a number nailed to the top, beginning at three hundred one. Conversations were going on behind each door that I walked past. Some conversations sounded benevolent while others sounded extremely malevolent. I did not know what this place was, but it appeared to be a waiting or holding place - for what, I was unsure. I tapped back into that quiet place in my mind, allowing it to guide me to where I needed to go.

I came to room three hundred three, which was eerily quiet. This was the only room that was silent. The truth is that quiet yet still voice, often silenced or left alone. Feeling confident this was the room I was looking for; I reached my hand out to knock on the door. When suddenly, the door opened with light that blinded me. I hunched over, shielding my eyes, when I could hear a soft, gentle voice speak aloud to me.

"Do not be afraid. Open your eyes," the gentle voice said.

Listening on command, I opened my eyes with ease and could remember being here before. The memories were quite patchy, but it was a place of total nostalgia. I knew this place, and I knew it quite well.

"Come closer," said the gentle voice.

I walked toward the center of the room, and a tall tree began making its way up from within the floor. The leaves were the most vibrant, brightest green I had ever seen, each leaf being trimmed in gold. Red and green apples hung from the tree by vines made of shiny gold.

Upon examining the leaves and fruit closer, I could see the gold veins that pumped life throughout each branch, stem, fruit, and leaf of this tree. The tree smelled of freshly cut apples and freesia flowers, a truly unique yet calming smell when paired together.

"Give me your hand," said the gentle voice coming from the tree.

A branch began to come down from the tree. I placed my cut hand on the extended branch. Gold blood from the tree started flowing into the cut on my hand and lifting me slowly to the top of the tree. A bed of white calla lilies with black stems formed where I was placed. These were the most intriguing flowers I had ever seen and made for the softest pillow.

The intoxicating smell induced me into a blissful slumber state where I was met by a beautiful goddess. She had long, straight white, cashmere hair, as pure as the first fallen snow. She had a white crown with amethyst stones of varying appearances all over it. An oval-shaped amethyst stone was housed in the center, with numerous square and circular stones covering the rest of it.

Her gown was made entirely of purple, white, and black calla lilies, all of which had gold stems. Her skin was the color of brass with the appearance of pure silk encapsulated in a glowing purple aura that surrounded her.

"You have come here to know the truth of many things. Have you also come prepared to know the price of *this* truth as well?" Her voice was very gentle yet echoed everywhere inside of me like surround sound.

"The *price?*" I asked in confusion.

"Yes, *the price.* Nothing is free, not even here. A price must always be paid."

"I come prepared to know the truth, and I accept what comes with this knowledge."

I could feel the glare from her eyes, the glare stared straight through me to my core. Her eyes began to change from an emerald green color to a murky, gray color.

"I know of your questions before you even ask them, and I will answer every single one of them. Before I do that, I must tell you a brief story first," she began.

I perked up, listening intently. Her voice was captivating and commanded all my attention. I was enamored by not only her appearance but also by her firm, yet gentle voice.

"There once was a group of candles that were all lit. One day; glowing brightly as they always had, God blew half of them out.

"'Why us? Why are we the only ones who are no longer lit any-more? Why did you take our light from us?'" One of the blown-out candles asked God.

"Only immortals know the difference between the dark, which forms the spiritual universe, and the light, which forms the ma-terial universe. How would you ever know what light is if I did not give you this experience of darkness? How would others know what darkness is, if there was never a distinction made?" God replied.

"Those candles gave birth to light and dark energies of this world and every other world in between. Neither energy can be destroyed; both energies can only be transmuted and constantly are. The lines can become blurred when things are looked at from the perspective of good versus evil. It is important to remember the candle story and the truth about energy. This will later become the answer to a question you did not even know you had," she continued.

She then began walking towards me, with every step she took leaving a trail of flower petals falling at her feet. A group of flowers began forming a chair for her to sit down in; enveloping her as if each one was acting as a personal bodyguard of hers.

"Join me," she said, pointing to the chair of flower petals coming together next to her.

I got up from the bed of flowers within the tree I was placed in and walked over to the newly formed chair of flower petals. As I sat down, the flower petals continued forming around me and felt soft, warm, and silky. A projection suddenly appeared at the center of us, displaying visual images that followed along with her story as she began talking.

"You never had an ordinary childhood because you are not ordinary. Your life was never meant to be ordinary, along with the experiences you've endured. These experiences gave you extraordinary abilities to hear, see, and feel things others cannot.

"They trained you, broke you, and forced you to recreate, time and time again. With each break came a new creation; one that was more fierce and agile than the last.

"You became smarter and savvier, and are now becoming a deadly weapon. A deadly weapon that will become an unstoppable force within the time to come. *Your* truth is that you are the leader of the Indygos.

"The Indygos were created and sent and created directly by the Divine Universal Mind, making them immortal by birthright. They preserve and maintain the balance between light and dark energies. Each Indygo having intrinsic abilities within them.

"The Divine Universal Mind more than understands what it takes to create not just a good leader, but a legendary one. A true, legendary leader that efficiently leads, maintains, and governs both energies through becoming one with the light and the dark.

"This requires a certain kind of discipline, one that takes several years to establish. You have never been one to step up to the plate of leadership; usually being the first one to volunteer another. Yet you are the only one who can bring balance in a delicate, calm, and sanctioned harmony. You run from your leadership, yet, your leadership runs after you, creating this nonsensical game of cat and mouse chase.

"The Indygos were created with the Diving Universal Mind's DNA, representing the elements from which all things are created; air, water, fire, and earth. Indygos populate fifteen percent of earth's current population, most unaware that they are different, and having these certain special abilities. Yet, they are aware there is something vastly different about them that sets them apart from the rest.

"This encryption within their DNA is how you will find them and reach them. You will find that what is ahead of you is unlike anything you have ever experienced before. Thus, Emanii and King were also strategically selected to accompany you on this journey as your descendants from the Holy Realm from which you come. Emanii is the goddess of the spiritual waters and King is the god of warfare from the spiritual realm.

"The truth you *seek* predates thousands of years ago and is always the most difficult to accept. An agreement was made with inexplicable dark energy known as the 'Serpents,' or the lower kings; to exchange advanced knowledge of technology, information, and equipment with humanity for its evolvement. Humanity was then seduced by this intelligence and allowed interbreeding and cohabitation to occur.

"With the interbreeding and cohabitation, a treaty amongst the two was then created. This treaty then only allowed for the interbred bloodlines to become the elected and ordained officials within all positions that run, rule, maintain, and control the world. This ultimately deprived humanity of its birthrights to exercise personal free will always.

"What humanity did not know was that The Serpent species had a hidden Draconian agenda, one with many ulterior motives that solely seeks to control, enslave, dominate, and eradicate mankind through whatever means necessary. All evils, which seek to destroy mankind, are created through and by The Serpent species. They disperse henchmen that are responsible for executing their orders, per their hidden agenda.

"Artificial intelligence is gaining more and more momentum by the second. This relationship predates more recently within this past century. This second evil comes with the acquisition of the advanced knowledge and technology supplied by the serpent species. A.I. will become one of the worst evils known to man due to it being so vastly spread out amongst the entire civilization of humanity.

"Humanity has allowed A.I. to enter their homes, and their daily lives; it slowly removes their ability to think for self, operate for self, and seek self. Thus, removing all individuality to think, create, feel, and know the things required for their evolvement. AI has had the pleasure of endless time to sit back, observe, and watch humanity for almost over a century. They have been programming humanity, removing any sense of self, and the ability to think and choose for self.

"This brings us to the third evil, and possibly the most threatening to humanity, which is humanity itself. Humanity has abetted in reckless acts against itself since the beginning of time. Entering harmful, cataclysmic disasters, one right after the other. History has shown time and time again that the habits and recitals of humanity have not evolved, but have backslidden to a point where evolvement has become almost impossible.

"Chaos has erupted globally, confusion about the identity of self has set in, and humanity looks to every other place, rather than self-reliance to solve their issues. There are wars erupting all over the world. The stories of endless hunger, famine, drought, and pollution continue to take over the world. Humans have worked diligently at destroying the earth itself, the very planet required for their survival.

"This was all a part of the Serpent's hidden Draconian agenda and plan which was interweaved through all things on earth, no matter geographical location. This dark energy disrupts the balance so significantly that if balance is not restored and maintained, humanity and every other thing living as you know it, will only exist through memories of doom and failures.

"Light is a requirement for all things living. Thus, designer human robots will be all that is left, serving as a distant memory of what once was. Preserving life, anywhere within the universe, will become impossible. Darkness will ensue everything within its course and the light that forms, shapes, and sculpts everything within the darkness will cease to exist. Massive implications will be created that impact more than humanity, but all life in and of itself."

A tear instantly fell from my eye, falling on one of the flowers I was sitting on. Her words and the images she showed to me were dark and empty. These words and images will haunt my nightmares for a very long time to come. While I felt an amass of sorrow and pain, I was also filled with anger, rage, and confusion. I knew something had to be done on a cosmic level.

"I told you the last part would be the hardest," she said. "Prepare yourself. This next one is going to sting even more. The price for the information you were given will cost you the most."

She then put her head down and I could instantly feel her sadness. All I could think is, *FUCK! What have I done?! What have I accepted?! What is this price she keeps referring to?!*

"I asked if you were prepared for what the price would be for the information you seek. What has been said, cannot be unsaid. What has been heard, cannot be unheard, and what has been seen cannot be unseen. What has started cannot stop. You asked, and I provided, now you will pay the price. That is the way this whole thing works. You know this far too well, my child," she said, interrupting my thoughts.

"I do and I understand. What do I owe?" I asked reverently.

She let out a loud rumbling laughter.

"You will find out soon," she said, instantly disappearing into her flowers.

I woke up to the tree branch gently lowering me back down to the ground. As I stood up, the tree went back into the floor and the cut on my hand had vanished. I grabbed my candle to light the way back. I closed the door to the room I had entered, and a window magically appeared and began to open. I climbed through the opened window and within the blink of an eye, I was back at the beach.

It was morning now, and the sun was beginning to rise. I needed time to process everything I had just taken in. I gathered my things and began making my way toward the house, in deep contemplation of what I was just shown. There was no way to make sense of the things I was just told and shown, and there was also no way to prepare or make sense of what was to come.

All I could do was hold my breath and try to mentally process what I had just taken in, to the best of my ability; having faith that my steps would become more clearly defined in the days ahead and ordered.

~ 5 ~

CHAPTER FIVE:

Phase I. - Awareness

Ignorance is bliss...
Knowledge is pain...

Somewhere in the middle, you find awareness. Within this activated state of awareness, you begin to realize you were never buried at all.

You were planted and now you are growing roots. These new roots are connected to the knowledge that rooted you there.

It is here – in this state of awareness; you realize you were put there to grow, evolve, and to become.

The 'who' part being up to you.

A couple of weeks passed since I returned from our vacation. I was still angered and feeling conflicted about what I was shown and told. I entered a deeply disturbed state and could no longer function the way I used to. The more I thought about the things I was told and shown, the more I realized absolutely nothing is as it appears to be. It was as if I had entered some kind of horror show I could not wake up from.

I wanted more than anything to unsee what I had seen and to un-hear everything I heard, but I could not. No matter how hard I tried, I simply could not. Those images, along with her words, were burned and etched into my memory. This information was interfering with my day-to-day life on a massive scale. I did not know how to get things back on track from here.

I called my friend Jenayah and talked to her for a while to take my mind off things and get caught up with recent events. An old high school friend of mine named Antonio was randomly brought up. It reminded me of how we used to hang out all the time after school. We would talk about everything from girls that liked him, to guys that liked me. It made me wonder how we fell out of touch and why we no longer kept contact.

His mom was very strict and kept him on a rather short leash. He was hardly ever allowed out to do anything after school. His mom did not seem to like him hanging out at my house after a while of us hanging together. I was never quite sure of what happened or what changed. However, on some level, this was understandable from a parent's perspective. I was probably considered a cautionary tale for most parents due to my rebellious attitude and trying times at home.

Curiosity striking an all-time high one afternoon, I decided to give him a call. I was not sure if he had the same phone number after all these years, but it was worth giving it a try. I could hear ringing, and suddenly on the third ring, a deep voice answered.

"Hello?" said the deep voice that answered.

"Hey, is this Antonio?"

"Yes, who is this?"

"It's me, Cam."

Before I could get anything else out, he suddenly blurted out,

"Oh my God, Cam?! How have you been? I have been looking for you!"

"Why, for what?" I have always been a "straight to the point" type of girl. It struck me as odd that he was looking for me at the same time my curiosity was also searching for him.

"Hahaha!" He laughed. "I have always admired your ability to cut straight to the chase, no matter how awkward the situation is. This may sound strange, but over the past week, you have come to my mind often. I am not sure why, but maybe that is the reason for you finding your back way to me."

"Interesting you mention this. I have been running into a lot of these strange, almost pre-arranged, situations lately. I am starting to ponder the meaning of these situations myself."

"Hey, whatever the reason, I will take it. How can I be of help to the great Cam?" he responded eagerly.

"I just wanted to see how you were doing. I was talking to Jenayah and she brought you up. It made me think back to how we used to hang out and talk all the time back in the day. I could use that friend to talk to and hang out with right now. I need to bounce some information off someone who has a differently wired mind than me or what I am used to."

"Fly out to see me. I will send my private jet to get you. I will send you the details. Just be there. It will be good to see you again, Cam. We have much catching up to do."

I guess this was non-negotiable as he hung up with that. I thought to myself, *this may be exactly what you need.* Once he sent me the arrangements, I planned for my kids to stay at their friend's houses for the weekend, and I flew out early that next morning.

I had never been to Seattle, Washington before. I had only driven through it with my ex-husband when he was prior military, and we were headed to the housing they set up for us in Everett. From what I remembered it was always raining there, which was beautiful the first couple of days, but it got old quickly and kind of depressing.

We arrived on the roof of a facility that was boarded by mountains. It looked like some kind of super top-secret military or government office. It was all gray and looked like it was made of cement. The windows were black and the only color was the blinking lights on top of the roof and around the building. I was instructed to head towards the garage area, where there would be a car waiting for me.

As I headed back to the garage area, fluorescent blue head-lights of a BMW became apparent in the distant background. As I approached the headlights, I could see a tall figure standing in front of them. It was Antonio. Even though we are now in our thirties, he did not look like he had aged more than five years since the last time I had seen him.

He stood well over six feet tall and was wearing a crisp pair of fitted blue jeans, a white t-shirt with a black hoodie over top of it. A nice fresh pair of white air force ones, and a black and red OSU buckeyes hat. Handing me a bouquet of white roses he said,

"I remembered how much you used to love white roses."

"I still love white roses. Thank you, Antonio, and thank you for the pleasant flight. I have never flown private before. It was a beautiful and serene experience."

"That was the plan," he said, grinning ear to ear.

"Cute, very cute. Well, I like this plan and really do appreciate everything you have done for me. You are amazing! I have missed you, my old friend!" I reached up and gave him a big warm hug. "Okay that's enough of this mushy stuff," I said, making my way over to the passenger door.

"Wait a minute, hold it!" He yelled.

I stopped dead in my tracks.

"I know it has been a while and I also know how you can be. But, while you are here, you are on *my* terms. You will allow me to show you chivalry, which is NOT dead, contrary to popular belief."

He began walking in my direction towards the passenger side door. He opened the door and gestured for me to get in.

"Thanks, Antonio."

I kissed him on his cheek before getting in. I appreciated his friendship more than he knew. It had been a while since I had been in the presence of a real man in quite a while, and it felt nice. Contrary to popular belief, I didn't want to always be in control, I just usually always had to be. It was nice to put my guard down, even if only for a few days or just for these few moments.

He walked around the car and got in. Whatever cologne he was wearing smelled divine and the car was filled with the pleasant and intoxicating aroma.

"How are your kids?"

His question suddenly interrupted my thoughts and the rabbit hole they were going down, thankfully.

"Great! They are bigger than me now."

"Everyone is bigger than you," he responded with a laugh.

"Hey! I cannot help that I'm vertically challenged."

"True story... Well... How does it feel to be smaller than your children?"

"Alright, comedian. That is enough. I am small but I am fierce!"

"I do not doubt that at all, Ms. Wolf... I do not doubt that at all..."

The scenery was beautiful. There were tall buildings everywhere, with stores and gas stations on every corner. I liked this little setup; everything was within a very close proximity. We pulled into a garage that went underneath his home. He had several other cars and trucks lined up within this garage.

"Wow, a different car to drive each day of the week?" I asked.

"Most of these were gifts."

"Wait, what?"

"Yeah, I only bought a few of these, the rest were given to me as gifts. The black BMWs over there are company trucks. You are welcome to use whichever vehicle you would like while you are here. Come on, I will show around and where you are sleeping."

We walked over to elevator. He pressed the button that had a 'P' at the very top of the buttons. A few short moments later, we were on the penthouse floor from the garage. There were only two doors on this floor, one had a 'Penthouse' plate on it and the other door had a 'Guest Penthouse' plate on it.

"Get settled in. I will be back in about an hour."

He opened the door to the guest penthouse room and had his assistant bring my things in from the flight. I headed in and put my things away in the dresser next to the bed. I opened the curtains in the room to let some light in. Everything in this room was immaculate, everything in a very precise order. There were nice toiletry items in the bathroom with fresh linen sitting out ready for use. I gathered a couple of items to take a nice, hot shower.

I don't know if it was the steam from the shower or just the jet lag, but I laid down on the bed afterward to cool off for just a moment will and was out like a lightbulb minutes later. I woke up in a dark room with the curtains still open, how I left them. It was thunder storming, rain pouring against the windowpane.

I searched around for my phone, trying to determine how long I had been out. The phone lit up to show that it was 8:19pm. Feeling like I had been asleep forever, I got up and put some clothes on, and brushed my teeth. I walked out to the guest kitchen area where I found a note that read:

"Come find me in the penthouse suite when you wake up.
-Tony"

I went out to the penthouse suite door and knocked. As Antonio opened the door, I was instantly met with something that smelled incredible!

"What is that I smell?" I asked. I was starving!

"Something I know you will like and something that was easy for me to cook. It's storming bad out there right now, and I didn't know how long you would be asleep. We gotta eat, so... Hopefully, you like it! What can I get you to drink?"

He was so adorable! This was truly admirable and humbly appreciated on many levels. Even after all the years I was married, I had never experienced this kind of treatment. It was refreshing. Especially after everything I had gone through over these past couple of years.

"I would love something to drink. If you have any root beer or cream soda, I will seriously love you forever!"

"Say less. I will be right back."

He took off toward the kitchen. I looked around and sat down on the oversized, L-shaped black sofa closest to me. He came back in and handed me a crisp, cold can of cream soda.

"Thank you, thank you."

He smiled at me and nodded his head. He flipped the switch up that was above the fireplace and it became lit. He hit another button and the TV began emerging from the décor it was previously hidden in.

"Make yourself at home." He said as he handed me the remote and headed back into the kitchen.

I flipped through the channels and put on a documentary that caught my interest. I curled up in the couch's corner with a blanket and the cream soda he brought me. He returned sometime later with food trays, and our food. He made us grilled steak, sauteed potatoes with onion, and bell peppers. With nice, crisp steamed broccoli on the side.

"This looks delicious, Antonio! Thank you. You have truly gone above and beyond, all for someone you haven't seen or talked to in years."

"You're welcome," he said as he sat down next to me. "I know I haven't seen or talked to you in years, but you said you needed that friend from high school to talk to. And while that friend from high school does not live down the street anymore and now lives in Washington, I wanted to recreate that open space. I know you would have done the same for me."

"Of course, without a question." I replied.

He looked over at me and placed his hand on mine and said,

"Same, without question."

I smiled at him and could feel my eyes getting watery. This was the most extravagant thing anyone had ever done for me in my entire life. To him, it was just helping a friend out in need. To me, this meant the world.

"You do not have to always have your guard up with everyone. Not everyone is a bad guy. Now, enough of the guarded thoughts! Dig in and let me know what you think! I put my heart into this and added an extra side of healing and love just for you!"

He used his hand to wipe the tear that fell from my eye and gestured towards the plate. I smiled and took a bite of the potatoes.

"Well, what do you think?!" He excitedly asked.

"This is phenomenal! The flavor is amazing and these potatoes are so tender. They just melt in your mouth like butter. I need the recipe for these." I simply could not get enough. I tried the rest of the food he made and everything was cooked to absolute perfection! "What did you do, take cooking classes or something?"

"I am glad you like it. I honestly would have been kind of pissed if you didn't. I hand-selected these steaks myself! I remembered how you always used to talk about how you would kill just to have a steak and potatoes with a side of broccoli. Back in the day to you, this was living good!" he said and began laughing.

We reminisced about our high school days over our steaks with so much laughter. I had briefly forgotten all about my troubles. It was like we were back in high school and for that moment, I had no worries, just the enjoyment of his company. Once we were done eating, he took me on a tour of his home. It was an incredible layout, the perfect bachelor pad!

There was a button for everything and a screen in every room that controlled the heating, cooling, intercom system, music, cameras, you name it, there was a button for it. Looking around at all the tech stuff, I could see how the Serpent plan was integrated throughout everything. They were always watching, always listening, always there. I looked over at Antonio.

"What if I told you that on the other side of these lenses, eyes are looking back at you? Would you then have these screens in every room?" I asked him.

"What if I told you I already knew there are eyes behind those lenses and I only allow them to see what I want them to see?"

"How is that possible? They are in every room. What about your phone? Do you censor that too?"

"My, my, little grasshopper. You are quite curious. I will make you a deal. I will tell you my secret if you tell me yours," he replied, with a grin as big as ever on his face.

"What secret?" This was a loaded question. If I told him the truth about many things, he would probably have me committed to an insane asylum somewhere.

"Well, something brought you out here to me. Probed the curiosity that sparked the phone call you made to me. Something so strong, you came to my mind frequently within the past week. I am not sure what this secret is, but something is telling me you do."

"If I told you the truth about anything that's went on lately, you would think I'm legit certifiable."

"Try me," he said, his voice as calm as ever. "Do not forget, I own a software company. What others see as crazy, in most cases, I see as interesting. Something brought you here, to me, Camryn. What was or is it? What's going on?"

I started from the very beginning; I told him about the accident, the visions, the dreams, the channeling; I told him everything, every single detail, and he listened, never interrupting once. I felt like a huge brick had been lifted from my chest. I had finally gotten it all out, and maybe even got it out to someone that could help me.

I let out an immense sigh of relief and fell back onto the couch. Antonio looked at me in a way he had never looked at me before. I did not know what this look was or what it meant, but I suddenly felt reassured. Reassured that I was exactly where I was supposed to be for reasons I would later learn. We sat there in silence for a few minutes.

I think we were both paralyzed in thought at everything I had just told him. Hell, even to me, it sounded like something straight out of a science fiction movie. Suddenly, he reached over and grabbed my hand.

"There is something you need to know. There is something I need to tell you, but I do not want you to be scared," he said.

"Okay, now you are scaring me. Just tell me, there should never be any secrets between us."

"No, no. It is nothing like that. You do not need to fear me. I just want to tell you something in an open forum, like what I provided you. No judgments, no negative thoughts. Only listen, okay?" He squeezed my hand as if we were making some kind of deal.

"Of course, Antonio, just tell me."

"Back in high school, you were the perfect girl for any guy to have on his arm. You are extremely beautiful with the body of an amazing goddess and the brains to match. On top of that, you are completely down to earth; you have the homiest vibe and could talk to anyone in the room. What was not to love?!

"You always spoke your mind and never seemed to have a filter on what came out of your mouth. You said what everyone else was thinking but was too scared to say. You became an idol to most people that met you, and still are a legend to this day.

"You always had your shit together, even back then, and you knew it, even if you did not realize you knew it. Everyone could see this, not just me. I used to think to myself, a woman like this is going places in life. You have the most beautiful smile I have ever seen, with the personality to match.

"You truly were the light of my eyes and still are, for many reasons. My mother knew this and it scared her. As you know, you were most parents' nightmares, being a complete rebel; but I saw something my mother couldn't see. However, she also knew I didn't just like any kind of girl, so if I liked you, she realized it was probably something serious.

"A couple of nights before our graduation, I attempted to muster the courage to tell you how I felt. But that night before the grad-uation ceremony, I had a dream about you. The dream showed me the outcome of events that would happen once I told you and it also showed me the outcome of events that would happen if I said nothing at all.

"Both outcomes inevitably involved a car crash, but only one of those crashes you survived. The thing is, the dream I had that night that showed me all of this and it felt so real to me that it made me sick, physically sick."

"Is that why I couldn't find you on graduation day and why we stopped talking all of the sudden?"

"Yes. I did not have it in my heart to tell you about my dream, and the little courage I had to tell you the truth about how I felt was gone. I thought I could have somehow prevented the accident by not telling you the truth about how I felt; I would rather have you here and alive than not here at all. But wait a minute, that is not even the strangest part of the dream, though. Are you ready for this?"

"Yes, tell me already. Tell me everything!"

"Well, the strangest part of the dream was the constant gold glow that followed you everywhere. It was almost as if you were royalty or

"After the car accident when you died, it showed you becoming a Phoenix bird flying towards the sun. You were something more, something else, something different from me and everyone else I knew.

"Something so pure and divine, I honestly did not feel worthy enough to even approach you anymore. I still don't feel worthy enough to have you sitting in my house right now, BUT I believe you were led here for many reasons. Reasons I feel all tie in with what I was shown back in high school when I saw the truth about what you are and who you will become. That gold glow represented royalty in my mind and the form you took was something out of this world.

"So...needless to say, I do not think you are crazy at all. I feel somewhat validated now, several years later, in knowing that the girl I went to high school with really is the Goddess from my dream! I feel I finally have closure, honestly. That whole situation threw me off for quite some time, but I always thought about you and wondered how you were doing. I had my ways of keeping tabs on you over the years."

He was fidgeting with a pen he had in his hand. I could tell he was nervous and that it took a lot of strength for him to tell me this. I leaned over and gave him a soft kiss on his cheek. We somehow stayed up until four in the morning just talking and reminiscing about old times. It felt good to be in his company.

It was almost as if we had picked right up where we left off in high school. I never had much of anything to call home growing up. But this feeling right here, with him, at this very moment, felt like home to me. I felt only a calming sense of peace and tranquility when we were together.

The combination of the rain, his wonderful smell, and the fireplace became the perfect recipe for deep soul sleep. Being with him felt like a dream, a really good dream I did not want to wake up from. I fell asleep in his arms that night, the place that felt the closest to home.

*****

As I was drifting off and entering my dream state, I arrived back at the lake. I could see Pooh off in the distance near the swing she loved swinging on. She was wearing an adorable yellow dress that had pink and white flowers all over it. She was skipping her way over to me.

"Did ya miss me?" She yelled.

"You know I did!" I yelled back.

"This is the happiest we have seen you in quite some time. Your soul is glowing!"

"I like how I feel when I am around him. I didn't want to drag him into all of this but I'm glad I did. I feel relieved in many ways."

"I think it is too late for that. Besides, he is a part of the plan. Just remember to trust the process. Let how you feel serve as an internal compass or indicator that you are on the right track and headed in the right direction. There is nothing wrong with feeling good and relaxing. You do not have to figure out how to save the world in a day!" She suddenly bursts into laughter.

"Thanks, Pooh. I needed that. I am glad you came to see me. It has been a while."

"I know, right! We have much to discuss. First thing is first, I bet you thought this was all a coincidence that Jenayah brought Antonio up, huh?"

"Wasn't it?"

"Not at all. Remember, there are no such things as coincidences. Everything that happens to you is happening for you, and through you, to achieve the goal. The reasons you were brought to him, is that he not only has some information you need, but he will also become a resource for you at a later point in time.

"Be diligent about the time you spend with him this weekend; he will show you a lot, and bring you to even more. Hold tight to this one, he is good for you and only houses pure intentions. However, you must remain focused and vigilant; not allowing distractions or additional liabilities to take precedence over our matters, which must always remain the first and top priority for you. Keep in mind, always, your mission."

I nodded my head in acknowledgment. I knew I did not have time for a relationship right now. I did not know if I would ever get into another serious relationship, but what I knew was that time was not now.

"Your channeling of the truth itself was the first step in the process of your rebirth. You are now in phase one of the process. The veil has officially been lifted. You will see, hear, touch, taste, and feel everything differently now. The heightened senses you have experienced since leaving the hospital will become even more heightened over the days to come.

"You will see the truth in all things, people, situations, circumstances, animals, food, politics, religion - absolutely everything. You will also be able to see the other dimensions around you; the people, places, and things within it. This will be your blessing and your curse to bear.

"You must not be afraid of what lies ahead, for you are always protected, guided, directed, and backed by a higher power. All your steps have been pre-arranged, and are anointed and protected. You must trust the process and listen to the voice inside of you.

"It is important to remember who you are and what the real truth is; for many distractions and tactics will be deployed to throw you off their trail. They know you are coming, but they currently do not know who you are. Use this to your full advantage in the days to come, as you will not be as fortunate to have anonymity in the days ahead."

"How would I lose my anonymity? I work for a bank; I fly under the radar and hardly talk to anyone anymore."

"You are only seeing what is currently in front of you, not what is ahead. To see what is ahead, you must think ahead. You must project yourself daily to the future and work from there. Anything you create within the mind's eye will be realized in a tangible form. You, if anyone, know this all too well. You just forget to apply it to yourself sometimes. This brings me to my next point.

"Your processes you currently use for thinking will also change, as you have never thought for yourself before. Your mind will be introduced to new synapses that will create and trigger the transmutation process within your body. Once the transmutation is complete, you can no longer operate within the same capacity you have once operated within.

"You will be in complete control of all your thoughts, words, and actions for the first time in your life. Displaying true free will. With this newfound freedom, it is important to note that the only counsel you may seek is within. You may never venture outward to seek information.

"If you do, you will fall prey to their deployed tactics. Always, always remember, The Kingdom of Heaven is inside you and can be found all around you. You must remember that, always, no matter what. Never doubt yourself, and to yourself, always be true."

She then disappeared without a trace, her words never leaving such a sharp sting as they have now. I went over to the lake and put my feet in the water. I needed to take some healing with me before whatever these changes are would occur.

As I moved my feet around in the water, I could feel another presence there with me. An unfamiliar presence, one that was new to me. I could feel the presence getting closer and closer. As I turned around and looked over my shoulder, I could see what appeared to be the figure of a wolf out of the corner of my eye.

The wolf that was slowly and calculatingly approaching, had come closer and was now sitting in the grass, not moving. I turned back around facing the lake, wondering what this visitor meant and what it had to tell me. Since the wolf continued to sit there, no longer approaching, I figured I would go up to it and introduce my-self. I got up and began walking slowly in its direction. A thought suddenly dawned on me to try talking to the wolf.

"Who are you, and why are you here?" I asked to the cautious wolf.

The wolf got up and began to come out of the shadows, walking closer in my direction. This wolf was huge, over seven feet tall! Its eyes were the color of a bright, yellow gold that glowed like head-lights in the dark. It was a gray wolf that had an illuminating red crown that went around its head. Nothing like anything I had ever seen before.

The energy that radiated from this majestic beauty was energetic and youthful, yet extremely wise and calculated. Once directly in front of me, the wolf stopped. I could tell from the cuts on the nose, that this wolf's been through battles too. I reached my hand out to touch its nose.

"You are so beautiful," I said.

The wolf sat down and lowered its head. As I touched its nose, the wolf looked into my eyes, and I looked back into its eyes. We sat there for a moment in genuine awe of each other, when I realized I knew these eyes. We had a history together, a lot of history. I have seen these same eyes so many times before, it's almost like....

In an instant, I am jolted awake. I lie there with my eyes wide open. I was not ready to leave the lake; I needed more answers. I could not get the wolf's eyes out of my head. It was as if they were burned into my memory bank. Even when I closed my eyes, those golden embers were all I saw. Why couldn't I remember where I know these eyes from? Where did she come from and why was she there? I looked around, suddenly remembering where I had fallen asleep.

"There she is. You looked so peaceful. I did not want to wake you." His voice was always so calming and soothing. I sat up.

"How long have you been awake?" I asked him. He looked like he had been up for some time.

"Not too long, but long enough to check some emails and make some calls. Did you sleep okay? It looked like you were having some interesting dreams."

"Yeah, I slept great. That is the best sleep I've had in quite a while."

"Hmmm... Well, I made plans for us today, if that is okay with you? I want to show you around a couple of places and then take you out to dinner somewhere nice. Since this is the only full day we have together, I want to make the most of it. Let us not waste a single minute. Go and get dressed!"

"How exciting! Okay, I am going to go and get ready."

I headed back to my room to shower and change. About an hour later, I was given a grand tour of Seattle. I was shown the best places to eat, live, shop, work out, and hang out. I had a blast and ate so much that I could barely move. It was about six in the evening and we were headed downtown. We pulled into a parking garage, where he pulled into a spot that had a sign that read "CEO: Antonio Jasper."

"I want to show you something," he said.

We walked up to the elevators and once inside, he hit the button to the 20th floor. Once we reached the 20th floor, he used a special card key card to open the elevator doors. The doors opened, and there were two white couches facing each other in front of the doors with a silver center table that had various magazines all over it.

There was a reception desk along the wall that was made of glass and a matching chair, but was currently empty. We headed back to his office, which was in the very back, and required another swipe of that special card key to get in.

"Look at your phone," he instructed. I took my phone out of my purse and looked at it. I had no bars for service. "Go ahead, walk around, and try to find service." He said with a grin on his face.

I walked around his office corner to corner. No matter what area of the room I was in, there was no service. Suddenly, he bursts into laughter.

"No matter where you go in this room, you will not find service unless I allow you to find service," he said.

"Wow! Why? How could someone ever reach you in case of an emergency?"

"The office phone still works. My receptionist can also page me through her intercom system that comes directly back here to me if she gets a call." He walked around to his desk and began booting up his systems. I sat down in a chair in front of his desk.

"I find I work better and have clearer thoughts without the constant daily distractions and constant radiation exposure we are now all subject to."

"Radiation exposure we are *now* all subject to?" His statement threw me off.

"Nothing is as it appears to be. Trust me."

"What do you mean by that? You know I do not do well with hints, Antonio."

"Okay, listen. This recent pandemic is because of the extreme radiation caused by the 5-G network rollout. This 5-G network is not what you think, it was a major step in establishing the new world order (NWO). That vaccine people are getting has technology in it to track everything about you. All your conversations, your personal financial information, DNA, and health information, literally everything. It can even shut you down at any time it wants, literally.

"Kind of reminds me of that book in the bible, *Revelations*, when it talks about the mark of the beast and a barcode being implanted in their right hand or forehead. I thought it was a mythical story, but I was so wrong.

"There's nanotechnology placed in the vaccine that acts as a GPS tracking device and can shut down the host with the click of a button. This might not be a barcode the eye can see, but it is serving the same purpose, if you catch my drift? But, this isn't the mark of the beast the bible was referring to, that one is yet to come. This is just the preliminary workup to it."

"It all makes sense to me and clicks with the Serpent plan to annihilate life itself."

"Soon, they will require the vaccinations and proof of the vaccination history to be able to go anywhere. They are setting up camps all over the world to prepare for the NWO takeover coming. Look at this," he said turning his screen towards me. "This is really what is happening. You see this?"

He pointed towards the top of an image of the earth with layers of the ozone showing. There were holes burned through every layer. He then zoomed into different areas all over the world that had stacks and stacks of new construction project-style homes being built on land currently uninhabited.

"What does all this mean, exactly?"

"Well, those major icecaps that melted in the Antarctic recently are direct results of this 5-G rollout, on top of a mountain of other chaos getting ready to erupt. With the ice caps melting, there is no way to regulate our atmosphere. We are all subject to constant and daily radiation; soon to be walking around looking like chemotherapy patients with no hair.

"Those little prisons being thrown up are where humanity will be forced to live once the takeover happens. This came to me the other day, and I want you to have it." He took out a manilla envelope that was quite thick and sealed.

"I think you will find this of interest. When you have some time, read through it. There is a lot more information on what I just told you in there. Be careful not to share that information with anyone or to let anyone know you have it."

"I promise it's safe with me."

"Oh, that is just the beginning of my blessings. I figure, if I could not figure out what to do with it, I would pass it along to someone I felt could. I have a few boxes of things I am going to send with you tomorrow on your journey back home. There's so much material there, I'm sure it will take you some time to dig through, but when you do, let me know what you come up with."

I woke up the next morning feeling sad. I did not want our time to end. It felt like it was just beginning. I got myself together, packed up my things, and headed over to Antonio's room. He opened the door with the biggest grin on his face.

"I just got some good news! I will be flying with you, but getting dropped off in Denver. Have you ever been to the Denver airport (DIA)?"

"If I have, I can't remember."

"Oh yeah! More goodies are in store for you! Wait until you see it. I am curious what your thoughts are about it. I want to show you a few things that stood out to me. Make sure your phone is charged. You are going to want to take pictures and maybe even videos."

He grabbed his briefcase, and we headed out to his jet. A little while later, we arrived at the Denver airport and as we hovered closer, I noticed a very apparent and obvious swastika symbol directly over the runway.

"You see that, don't you?" He pointed to the grotesque symbol below us.

"I see it." I was scared to see the rest of what was to come.

"If you decide you want to keep looking around at other things once I go, that's more than fine. Just let my pilot, Enrique know when you're ready, and he will fly you the rest of the way back home," he said.

"You are amazing, Antonio. Thank you, again, for everything."

"No, thank you for blessing me with your company. This will not be the last of us. I have a feeling we will be spending a lot more time together. So, turn that sadness into happiness. This is just the beginning!"

As we walked around the airport, the first thing he showed me was the gargoyles that looked like demons over the baggage claim area. We then walked around and came across some highly disturbing images, they were everywhere, in abundance. I made sure I took pictures of everything we saw.

"This is the picture I wanted to show you," he said as we approached a gigantic mural on the wall. "I have to take off, but let me know what you think." We gave each other goodbye hugs, and he walked off to his destination. "I will miss you, Ms. Wolf! Until next time!", he yelled as he walked through the hallway of the DIA airport.

I looked at the picture he left me at, of the gas-masked Nazi agent that had a dove at the end of its blade. This was beyond sick, this was repugnant! There were slain children in the picture with a trail of weeping mothers who also appeared slain, assuming by the Nazi demon and the sword shown in the picture.

They were being sent to something like a conveyor belt. I couldn't help but to think, *who the fuck puts this garbage on airport walls to a major airport facility, where families fly in and out of?! What the hell are they hiding here, in plain sight?!*

All the sudden, I felt an extreme amount of heat coming up from my stomach and into my chest. Then from my chest into my neck, where it then went straight to my face. I was infuriated and it was becoming harder to conceal. I needed to get out of here. Whatever energy was being housed here was setting me off, literally. I looked over at Enrique. He took one look at me and nodded his head.

"This way, ma'am."

I was happy to be leaving this place and felt a major sense of relief the moment my feet touched the floor of the plane. I sent Antonio a text that said:

"I have no words for what I've just seen."

I looked out the window as we began departing and knew I was embarking on dark territory. Dark, uncharted territory, I was unfamiliar with navigating. My phone buzzed. It was a text from Antonio that read:

"... And sadly enough, that is just a tiny little sliver. When you get home and get a moment to yourself, look at the stuff I sent with you. I truly believe you will find the information there useful for your future endeavors - whatever they may be and wherever they may take you. I am always here if you need me. Remember that."

I looked out the window of the plane, down at everything that was becoming tiny little ants. I put my head back on the seat, kicked my feet up, and put my earbuds in. I cranked some music loud enough for me to drown out my thoughts and closed my eyes; preparing for the dark things I knew were sure to come.

~ 6 ~

CHAPTER SIX:

Phase II. - Acceptance

There's hidden power in the truth, that is why it is the most
desired attribute but seldom found.

Truth and acceptance are two very different concepts. One
requires you to receive and the other makes no demands at all.

When you combine truth with acceptance, that's when the real
magic happens.

However, with one knowing and accepting the truth, it also
becomes a realization that no-good deed goes unpunished.

A few days after I had gotten back home, I decided it was time to go through the things Antonio sent home with me. Before opening any of the boxes, something inside of me was warning I would never be the same again. I knew there would be no going back the second I decided to open Pandora's box. I could suddenly feel chills running down my back.

I opened the first box, which contained several file folders full of information. There were several emails, FBI and CIA docs, pictures, and other various forms of intel dating back thousands of years. I had no idea how long it would take me to comb through this information, so I pulled everything out and began making piles, grouping all similar information together. Once I had the piles grouped into their rightful category, I was left with exactly three piles.

I began digging through the first pile of folders I labeled, "Serpents." There were several government documents supporting different UFO landings along with their coordinates, spaceships, and the engineering of them, as well as a detailed analysis of their nanotechnology, aliens, and the study of their kinds (there were quite a few).

There were documents explaining time travel locations, demonic portals, and centers geographically placed around the world that were hidden gateways to travel from one realm to another. I could not believe what all I was seeing. The pictures provided of these things referred to as the "reptilian" and "serpent" species were the stuff straight out of nightmares!

Apparently, this reptile/serpent species goes way back before the time of the Garden of Eden. There were quite a few documents on something called the "Babylon Working" ritual, which was a portal here on earth that unleashed a plethora of different evil spirits dating back to 1946. The two idiots who opened the portal were apparently unable to close it, and now we have open portals that lead directly to hell here in the United States and other various countries.

I knew I would need more time to start from the beginning, so I set this pile to the side and picked up the second pile of information. I labeled the second pile, "Satanists." For a second there, I did not think it could get any worse but I was sadly mistaken. Upon examining a few of the docs, I began to see correlations, too many to ignore.

I have always been an open-minded person, leaving the whole judging thing to God. But this shit right here – this was some very dark, sadistic, and twisted shit! My Spidey senses were going off with all kinds of alarms. As I continued combing through the papers filled with the most disturbing information I had ever seen in my entire life; I pulled out one of the papers that was apart of a covenant agreement and OH MY GOD, I will never be the same!

The title of this agreement was called, "The Secret Covenant." I wish I would have just stopped there, but I didn't. Something in me could not leave this alone or just walk away. This agreement had detailed information on how to carry out the plans for this N.W.O. and to keep it under wraps from the general public. Their plans were weaved and integrated into everything and included children. It included things like brainwashing, hiding, and lying about history all over the world, putting certain chemicals into our food and water supply; the list going on and on.

As I kept digging, I found the main group of Satanists who are carrying out this agenda in the present time through varying branches — the Freemasons. The other branches also within the

Freemasons, like the CIA, FBI, The Finders, Illuminati, etc., were responsible for child abductions, child trafficking, and child slavery, and that is just to name a few.

There were even code names assigned to their child harming missions, like "Pizza Gate." Various designers were also involved within these sick schemes, contributing to the funding and perpetuation of harming children, for their sick and twisted agendas. So many different people and entities were involved with this like record labels, various artists, bank CEOs, business CEOs, social media and news executives, and the politicians were in abundance with their involvement.

Every time a state-level case would be opened into one of these groups, the CIA would step in and demand the issue be swept under the rug and hushed. These sick groups all fictitiously operated as different entities but really were just one main entity executing the same plan. All mysteriously leading back to the first file folder of the serpents.

I moved this pile to the side, also noting that significant additional research is needed. I picked up the third pile labeled, "Evils of Man." Hesitant to look at anything from this pile; I mustered the strength. I began scanning through multiple docs showing detailed outlines for the COVID-19 hoax and how it tied into the Secret Covenant. There was another document titled "Internment and Re-settlement Operations" that detailed a plan to detain all civilians and place them into "camps."

One document led to one rabbit hole, which then led to another, and then another. It was endless. This was happening with every document I came across and then it hit me. These were not separate entities at all, they were the same entity pretending to operate as many, so people would never make the correlations.

There was a laundry list of debts owed to the federal government from other countries and what they were for. Some entries with descriptions were missing, but the overall exchange always appeared to be for weapons and artillery. All the documents seemed to overlap with one another. They were all a part of some major plan that either always was in place or has become a new plan.

I saw that since infancy, we have been programmed and guided. Programmed to think only inside of certain boxes, with intelligence being measured only within certain categories. We have been guided on how to think, feel, act, talk, interact, and behave. This programming has removed the ability to think for self, feel for self, and do for self.

It has removed the most beautiful attribute that makes us all human; which is free will and the right to choose our destiny. This plan was a detailed plan that was interweaved throughout everything. Even being interweaved throughout our educational system and what our children are being taught in school.

Using religion as currency rather than spiritual enlightenment; redacting information and changing it to fit their corrupt agenda. The governments all over the world is completely polluted along with all our media, music, designers, artists, and entertainment. Our healthcare being designed to kill us off by a certain age rather than do what it is supposed to do, which is to heal and make people better.

I began connecting the dots and sat there in silence, my soul in total anguish. I did not know how to mentally compartmentalize all of this and had no one I could go to for help. I laid back and thought back on the collection of things I had seen and been told recently and began crying uncontrollably at the thought that all of this was real and true. Exhausted in every category of emotion, I began praying for clarity and guidance, something I hadn't done in quite some time, and shortly thereafter was carried off to sleep.

*****

I suddenly appeared at the lake where Pooh was sitting with her feet in the water, humming a song. I walked over to her and slipped my feet into the water beside her.

"I know you have been exposed to a lot lately and you are having a hard time making sense of everything you have been led to. Trust that inner voice inside of you that always tells you the truth. While this information will be very hard to investigate, you must know this information you've been given is a tool for enlightenment.

"To understand what this darkness is, you must first peer behind the veil of this evil, to be shown the truth of what it truly is. You cannot go into a battle unaware of what and who your enemy is. Every great and victorious King and Queen has always understood the art of researching your opponent before engaging.

"This information you were given is just the tip of the iceberg and there is a lot more to come. You must prepare and armor yourself in truth. The days ahead will test you to your core and everything you hold sacred. The world is not what you think it is, nor are the people and the things you are experiencing. Remember all things the truth itself told you, and apply that wisdom and knowledge to what you find.

"Be very mindful of remembering the matchstick story. That story is more important than you think. You are being given a lot of information in a very short amount of time. All for necessary reasons. Trust, that the things and people you need will come in their due seasons, all completing the bigger picture for you.

"For now, you must confront the personal issues you have going on right now in your life that will soon consume you if left unresolved."

"What personal issues?"

"A bank," I replied and could instantly feel guilt and shame. I knew where she was going with this.

"Exactly and therefore, you know what must be done. You are either a part of the solution, or a part of the problem. Your choices represent not only who you are but also your leadership, and legacy. Choose what kind of leadership and legacy you want to leave behind, wisely. Your precise level of execution and ability to think outside of normal boxes will give you your edge. Trust in what is to come and accept who you are."

Just like that, she was gone and I was back to being alone. I got up, turned around, and behind me was the wolf I had seen the last time I had come here. The wolf was close enough to touch. I looked into her eyes and she gazed back into mine. As I continued looking into her eyes, it looked like the gold in them was swirling and moving, like that of lava.

I moved in to get a closer look, and the moment I did that everything around us went black. All I could see was her glowing eyes ruminating in the darkness. She was once close to me but was now distant. It was completely silent, with unintelligible whispers happening in the background. The whispers were all mingled together, making it impossible to understand what they were saying. I felt around, but there was nothing within reach.

"You have now reached the second phase of the process, which requires you to learn more about yourself. You are far more than you now know and can understand. Your perspective is limited to the things previously taught and learned through your prior programming. It is important to remember that all things go into the dark to be developed, shaped, and made new.

"Which is why you were brought here, to the abyss. You have been placed in a cocoon, so to speak, which will develop you for the next phases ahead. The only way to put things in proper perspective is to undo the previous programming that has been completed. Each level up requires a sacrifice from you. Do not be afraid of the dark, this is where all greatness is conceived and birthed," The wolf said, her voice coming in above the whispers.

Her eyes were moving from the distance, getting closer to mine. She was back within touching reach of me. It was strange, but whenever I was in her company, I felt as though I was at home. As if she was a part of me in some kind of way. I did not fear her, even though I had every reason to. All the sudden, a major surge of energy bolted throughout my body and I woke up covered in sweat.

*****

This time when I woke up, I felt different, like something in me had drastically changed. Like I was someone brand new. I rubbed my eyes and looked in the corner of my room and there was a figure sitting there in the chair by the window. I rubbed my eyes again to see if I was just seeing things, and the figure then stood up from the chair, heading in my direction.

"Who are you?" I asked, terrified.

The figure stopped dead in its tracks and then vanished. I rubbed my eyes again to see if the figure would reappear but it was gone. I hopped out of the bed and turned the light on frantically. As I turned back around looking toward my bed, I could see the figure of a black cat running across the room toward the bathroom. I followed the cat toward the bathroom, but it was nowhere in sight.

I searched my room and all around my bathroom, and could not find where the cat had gone. I began questioning my sanity at that point. *Who was the figure and where did the cat go?!* I thought to myself. *I know the wolf mentioned I was going into the second phase, but did I bring someone back with me from abyss? What in the hell is going on here?!* I looked over at the clock, it was now 4:37 am, leaving me about two hours before I needed to get up and begin my day at work with the bank.

As Pooh said in my dream, I was either a part of the problem or I was part of the solution. However, I could not be a part of both. I knew an important decision needed to be made. The sooner being the better. This job was controlling too much of me and my time. More disturbing than that, it was also controlled by people with hidden agendas and ulterior motives. I was so disgusted with everything I had taken in and knew exactly what I needed to do.

It instantly hit me, I needed to create a business that would bring people from all over the world to me. While also providing exponential earnings, I could use as leverage in the building and acquisition for the days ahead. I sailed away, creating my first preliminary business plan. I wrote everything down that I would later type up after running it by Antonio.

He has first-hand experience with starting his own business and owns one of the world's biggest Fortune 500 tech companies in the world. Certainly, he would have a plethora of knowledge I could use. First things first, I had handle things with my current job. It would be hard saying goodbye to all I know and the people I know, but I could not stay, not any longer. I knew too much and with knowing too much, much will be required.

The decision had been made it just needed the execution. I sent in my resignation notice first thing that morning. It felt amazing to be done! I was no longer concerned with things like competitions, accuracy, or other arbitrary semantics, that really didn't matter in the grand scheme of things. I liked this new me that woke up this morning with eyes finally wide open. This new me made confident moves no longer questioning the things I did, said, or thought.

I leaned on and relied upon that internal compass/indicator Pooh told me about to provide the answers in the areas I needed them. I then called Antonio, telling him the good news.

"You did what?!" He was shocked and happy all at once.

I could not help laughing at his response. I counted on this being the general response I would get from everyone I told. Anyone who knew me knew how dedicated I was to my work, and how many countless nights and hours went behind my work. This was one of the riskiest decisions I had ever made in my entire life.

"This was inevitable. Especially after reading some of the infor-mation from the files that you gave me. I can either be a part of the problem or I can be a part of the solution, but I cannot be a part of both."

"Well in this world, we are all a part of both the problems and the solutions, at one point or another. Only when we become aware of what exactly those problems and solutions are, can we align ourselves with whichever side we choose to be a part of. You cannot blame yourself for things you did not know, Cam.

"Once you know better, you naturally want to do better and become a part of the solution, no longer aligning yourself with the problem. Everything naturally attracts and aligns with your evolvement and the more aware you become of things, the more information, tools, and resources that become available to you."

"Gosh Antonio, when did you get so smart? You never cease to amaze me."

"So, tell me all about this business plan of yours. I want to know everything from start to finish."

I told him all about my new plans to own and operate a one-of-a-kind resort here in Florida, which I would then turn into a chain of resorts. It was the perfect venue for many paths I wanted to explore while also providing a perfect place to attract a global audience. This would be a one-of-a-kind resort that would offer many amenities, goods, and services you could not get elsewhere within this geographical market. The idea was amazing if I must say so myself. There was nothing else like it! It would be the first of its kind and the first of its class.

"Do you have funding in place? That is usually the biggest hiccup with business start-ups. If not, I volunteer to be your sole investor!"

"Antonio, are you serious?! I haven't worked up a complete budget just yet but we are talking a couple million, at the least."

"Yes, I am serious. I am pitched business ideas all day, every day. This is the first one I have heard in a long time that is actually well researched and thought out. Not to mention, I could hear the passion in your voice the entire time you were talking about it.

"The passion factor is more important than any other factor because it is the element that keeps you going even when you want to give up. You have a purpose Cam, and I would like to help you see it through. Get the complete final business plan, including the budget to me. Once I get those figures, I will have my attorney draw up the docs."

"I appreciate you, Antonio. Probably more than you will ever know," I said, with tears streaming down my cheeks.

"I got you, girl! I told you this back in high school, you did not believe me. Neither one of us came from much of anything but you looked out for me and I looked out for you. Nothing has changed; we were family then and we are still family now and always. Now get to that computer and start making this shit final! I have to get to a meeting, unfortunately, but we'll talk more later."

Excited about the wonderful news I had just received, I decided to take the kids out to celebrate this new chapter in our new beginning. A new chapter that would begin shaping the rest of our lives. I took them to one of the eat and play places where we played arcade games, ate tons of food, and talked about our hopes and dreams for the future.

We were happy, and it showed. As I looked at them, I realized these little people were just mini extensions of myself, and their father combined into these little unique packages I loved so dearly. When they spoke, I could see so much of my younger self in them and became instantly so proud.

They were beyond intelligent and closely examined life through so many lenses I had not previously considered. Their insight was refreshing, calming, and kept me down to earth. I thanked God for allowing me this second chance at life and promised to never take these moments for granted ever again. Later that night after the kids were in bed, I headed out to the backyard and turned on the bubbles in the hot tub.

It was the perfect night for some adult celebration! I was never much of a drinker, but I have always appreciated and partook in good ol' Mary Jane! It was such a beautiful and warm night with a slight breeze in the air. As I got into the hot tub, I could instantly feel the tension melt away. This was a moment of pure perfection. I closed my eyes and laid back, enjoying my Mary Jane along the way.

I reflected on the progress I had made in transitioning from who I was into who I am becoming. I could not believe the monumental progress I had made over the past few years, months, and days. I would be the owner of the newest, latest, hippest, and trendiest resort in southern Florida! This would become the perfect platform for me to use to reach people, and my fellow Indygos.

While I could not see all the details that made up the complete picture just yet, I knew everything was falling strategically into place. I quieted my mind and headed inside to shower and prepare for bed. I was too exhausted to do anything else this evening and couldn't stomach the thought of looking at any more of those documents.

I hopped in the shower and let the cool water run down my body. I closed my eyes, allowing the cool shower water to run over my face, when I could suddenly see the face of a man piercing through my mind. His face was familiar to me, as if I had seen it a million times before. He had dark brown skin with crystal clear, blue eyes. Eyes that pierced through my soul with recognition.

I instantly opened my eyes and looked all around the bathroom, confirming it was empty. Between him coming into my thoughts, seeing random figures, and cats around my house, I was questioning my sanity regularly, feeling totally certifiable at this point. I went to bed and fell asleep after eating almost a half bag of Cheetos and cuddling with my cat, Honey, for a while. I briefly wondered if he was also able to see the random figures that were appearing lately.

The next morning, I woke up with a splitting headache which was odd. I never usually got headaches at all, let alone a headache like this. I could barely open my eyes. The smallest beam of light made the pounding sensation increase in seismic waves throughout my head. I tried my best to squint and see the time, but the more I tried, the more my eyes watered and the pounding radiated throughout my head.

I did not know what was going on, but I knew I needed to go back to sleep. This kind of pain and the radiance of it was not normal. I took some Ibuprofen and laid back down in the bed. Once the Ibuprofen kicked in providing some relief, I was able to drift back to sleep. I was woken up a few hours later by Emanii coming in to check on me.

"Good morning Mom, I just wanted to check on you. It's like way past noon and you're usually up by now. Is everything okay?"

"Good morning, my baby. I'm doing okay. I just had a horrible headache earlier but it's gotten a little better since I took some Ibuprofen earlier."

I sat up slowly, opening my eyes.

"Mom! You need to go to the bathroom and look at your eyes," Emanii said suddenly.

I got up, making my way over to my bathroom and turned on the light. I let out a huge gasp and just stood there, staring in the mirror at my eyes. *I know these eyes;* I thought to myself. *I have seen these eyes before, many times, but where?* I sifted through my memory bank for any familiarities I could find and paused when I remembered the wolf's eyes from my dreams.

Her eyes were this same golden color my eyes now were. My skin glowed as if it were covered in a cloak of shimmery diamonds. My hair was also longer and a lot thicker than it was before. I wondered if this was the result from my random excruciating headache earlier. Emanii came over to me and gave me the tightest hug I had received in the longest time.

I could feel her concern coming through her hug, but I couldn't find any words to relieve her concern, as I was just as much in shock myself. I remembered Pooh telling me I would go through physical transformations and also wondered if this was a part of the cocoon effect the wolf was telling me about.

"Hey Mom, just know I love you and you can talk to me about anything."

"I love you too, much more than you'll ever understand."

I figured this was not something I could hide and even if I could, I wouldn't be able to for long. King was just as shocked as I was by the discovery of my physical changes. It was not something I could put into a logical explanation for either of them to comprehend. However, they both seemed to understand that not all things could be explained, including but not limited to my accident.

"I don't know what all this means and right now I don't think you do either. But what I do know is there is a higher power at work here." King sounding wise beyond his years.

"I couldn't agree more," I replied.

After our little chat, the kids went to pack their bags for visitation time with their father and I went to work. I did not want to think about the fact that my babies had to leave me for a few months but I understood they needed time with their father and his new family too. Even if they despised going every time. I sat down and began drafting my final business plan and figures.

Even though I could not quite see all the stairs within the staircase, I could see the first few steps I needed to take. I was growing more excited at the thought of being able to live my life on my terms, all while achieving the purpose I was sent back for. It was always my dream to build a life I did not need to retire from and now I was doing just that. I defied the statistics. I came back from the dead and now I'm here to live. Something I had never done until now.

I refused to live the way I was living before and did not come back here to live a miserable, mundane life. Almost six hours later, my final business plan was emailed to Antonio. I took a deep a breath in and let out the enormous relief of stress that had been building. I headed to the kitchen to grab a cold bottle of water and could see another strange figure standing in the corner.

Whoever it was appeared to have the shape of a woman. I stopped in my tracks, not knowing what to do. I closed my eyes and opened them back up and looked back in the corner where I could suddenly see her crystal clear.

"I didn't channel you, what are you doing here?" I asked.

"You and I are now connected on many levels you will not understand at this time. However, the portal is now open. Now that it is, we have open lines of communication flowing between us now and always." She began making her way over from the corner, into the light.

"I can see your new gifts are in perfect working order," she continued.

"What do you mean?"

"You had to channel me of your own free will to gain access and open the portal for us to communicate. You could only see and hear me if directly connected to me. Now, you can see me and hear me with no intervention. This is massive progress. We are proud of you and the progress you are making. You have come a long way, but still have a long way to go. Do you know who you are?"

Confused by her question, I replied, "I'm Camryn Wolf."

"No, that is the government name you were given at birth. That name is not *who* you are. Following your many births, you have been known by many names. Although, none of the names you were ever given came close to describing an eighth of who you really are.

"These titles, experiences, and lessons, are not who you are. They were all just many fragments forming who you are becoming. You are a rare form of combined energy that cannot be replicated or stolen, no matter the efforts.

"You have lived thousands of lives, never tasting death. Your beliefs, practices, and ideals are still practiced to this day all over the world. You are not someone who can be summed up with words, but if you dig deep into the recesses of your mind, you will discover the truth of who you are.

"Your experiences were no coincidence; they were pre-arranged for your evolvement. This includes your current experiences, which were prepared to complete a picture for you. You must discover who you are and once on that path, another door will become open to you.

"This door will only become open to you once you know the truth about who you are. There is someone who wants to see you and has a message for you. Due to certain limitations, access cannot be granted until the discovery of self has been completed. Do not be afraid to fly; it is your time and you're ready."

She then vanished, only leaving a few flower petals behind and a scent of freesia. I sat down and began thinking back to the things I had seen in my dreams, the places I had gone, and the physical transformations I had undertaken. I pulled out my phone and kept staring at the pictures of my totaled truck. There was so much I did not understand, but there was so much more I could finally see.

Things were beginning to come into focus with greater clarity than ever. Being forced to relive every detail and memory of all the lives I had lived before this one became a daunting process, but one that I knew would pay off in the end. The things I tried to forget were vital in understanding my true character because they showed the truth of who I am, even in my darkest moments. They revealed another side to me that showed I was resilient, fierce, and at times a necessary weapon.

Before I died, there were a lot of things I did not realize. I put off dealing with them to stop the pain and hurting. The things that were never mentally compartmentalized properly grew into demons. Those demons then grew big enough and started making demands of their own. Demands that become insatiable no matter the sacrifice.

Those demons took over my life and controlled everything within it until they killed me, or so they thought. With my resurrection came their death and everything they claimed to keep. I have learned that all things in life happen for a reason. There are no such things as coincidences. There are only the things that you do and the things you do not do.

At the end of every day, you are left with a result of the choices you have made from that day, and every other day you have lived before this day. Your actions become the defining characteristic of who you are and what you will become. I am nothing more than a series of my causes and effects. I understood this now, within every aspect of my life.

Going forward, all my actions will always line up with who I see myself becoming and the legacy I want to leave behind, only. I will no longer allow others to set and control my value, my faith system, my belief system, and my thought process. I am the swimmer that swims with the current; not the log that becomes carried away by the current. I am and always have been the one that is in control of my destiny.

I will spread my knowledge throughout the world with faith as the driving force, which will raise the consciousness of the personal truth hidden within all of us. We are all heroes of our own stories; the adventure lies in finding the truth, and freedom lies within accepting it. I accept my truth; I accept who I am and I accept who I am becoming.

I also accepted my purpose in being here and would honor and protect humanity at all costs. It has become my personal mission to not only expose the evils for all that they are, but to also prepare humanity for what is coming. There is so much beauty within life itself, so much freedom. To take that from humanity is to stop evolution and I will never stand by that. I am a fierce leader, leader of the Indygos – that is *who and what* I am.

~ 7 ~

CHAPTER SEVEN:

Phase III. – Allowance

The most brutal fact that one must face in life is that you will never get what you deserve.

You only get what you tolerate.

Selah, (pause and think on that)...

Several weeks later, the business papers were signed and the initial plans were underway. It was a Wednesday afternoon; Antonio and I were having our weekly business collaboration call when he brought up suggestions for public relations agents. He made several recommendations, but the recommendation that stood out the most was Mack.

Like us, Mack also came from nothing and built a successful empire himself becoming a well-known Public Relations influencer, one of a kind. He also did a lot of philanthropic work and came heavily recommended by Antonio. Since Antonio used him in the past and was familiar with him, I decided I would give him a try before attempting to solicit PR on my own.

Mack had excellent reviews online and was highly rated and recommended by his clients that posted reviews. I did not know any direct connections in the Miami area and could use all the new connections I could get. I sent Mack a text and let him know I had received his number from Antonio and was interested in seeing when he was available for a meet and greet to discuss potential plans for the PR effort needed for my resort, Indygos.

Mack got back to me within five minutes with the details of the location for our meeting later that evening. I booked a suite in Miami that was close to the beach, packed my bags, and hit the road. We met up later that evening at an elegant steakhouse winery in Miami. I was greeted at the door by a man who greeted me by name,

"Good evening, Ms. Wolf. Mr. Vasquez has a beautiful night in store for you both this evening. Please, follow me this way."

I followed him down the hall to a smaller table for two with a candle that was lit in the center of the table. Mack stood up and pulled out my seat for me.

"Here you are, Ms. Wolf." He said, gesturing to the seat he just pulled out for me.

"Nice, very nice. Is this how you treat all your prospective clients?" I asked with a smirk on my face. If this is what meetings would look like for me going forward, sign me up! I was used to meetings being held in stuffy conference rooms with even stuffier people, that repeated the same mundane nonsensical bullshit to pass the time. I appreciated the deviation from the norm. We were already off to a good start.

"Actually, no. Usually, I bring prospective clients to my office."

"Why is this meeting different?"

"Because you are different."

"How so? You do not even know me."

"I know enough, and what I know intrigues me. I wanted to provide an environment that would allow for an open discussion. An open discussion about your future and where I see things going in the PR realm of things, if you decide to give me a chance and show you how I can be an asset to you. First, can I get you something to drink?" He asked gesturing for the waiter to come over to the table.

"A lemon water would be excellent."

"You don't want a proper drink, like a glass of wine or champagne?"

"I am not much of a drinker, as a general. When talking business matters, I hold sobriety in high regard."

"I understand." He looked at the waiter and told him, "Two lemon glasses of water, please."

Looking back at me, Mack said,

"Antonio said you were a 'straight to the point', kind of girl. I can see this much is true."

"Some call it straight to the point; others call it blunt, I call it removing the bullshit and not wasting time. I appreciate removing unnecessary semantics and setting proper expectations upfront. The bottom line of business is simple - I want something from you, you want something from me. For us to make this happen, you need to understand me and I need to understand you."

The waiter returned bringing our lemon waters.

"Would you like more time to look at the menu?" The waiter asked.

"Yes. Please give us some time to decide. We have not had the chance to open the menu just yet." Mack replied.

Looking back in my direction, he said,

"You are indeed a woman who knows what she wants, so let me straight to the point."

He began giving his presentation on what he planned to do for the marketing efforts, party planning, social media, and press releases. He seems to know his stuff, also being quite the Casanova. I was impressed by his thorough presentation, and just like that, he was hired. I did not tell him that right away, I wanted him to sweat a bit.

"There is a party tomorrow night. You should come. Many people will be there who can help expand your network in the Miami area. I will text you the details."

"I will think about it. Send me a detailed workup on the PR plans covering every stage and we will get together again soon. I will speak with Antonio later this evening to confirm our arrangement."

We spent the next hour enjoying porterhouse steaks with an effortlessly good convo. I enjoyed talking to him and seeing his perspective of things. He made me laugh and took my mind off the disturbing information I was recently provided. At the end of dinner, Mack walked with me out to the valet and waited with me for my truck to be pulled around.

Once my truck arrived, I was sent off with more pleas to come to the networking party tomorrow night. His coy smile was trouble, and I was sure of it. Being surrounded by beautiful men all the time was no simple task, but easy to do when your mind is traveling a million miles a minute to different places all the time. But it was nice to have pleasurable experiences with beautiful people. Good conversation coupled with keen intellect were prize worthy and a rarity to find.

Before taking off, I sent Antonio a text to let him know the meeting was a success. It was such a warm and beautiful night and I was not quite ready to go back home just yet. The kids were with their father and the house just did not seem the same when they were gone. It was quiet and eerie without them there and in some strange way, I missed all the noise and did not know how to operate without it.

I spent a little time driving around the city, looking at the beautiful lights in this amazing, fast-paced city. Miami felt alive and when I was here in this city, I felt alive too! The cool, coastal colors complimented with the beautiful people always walking around, gave the city a homey feel. I decided to pull over and watch the sunset from the moon roof of my truck, right next to the ocean.

The smell of the beach and the sound of the waves always bring a calming and peaceful sensation to me. In this peaceful trance I was under, I realized there was a deeper plan developing in the background. One I was unable to initially see, for the forest being in the way of the tree. This plan that was developing in the background had always been there, developing and waiting on its own time to be deployed.

I always tried so hard to put together a plan for my life and every time I thought I finally had it all figured out, something changed. Here I am again with everything changing, none of which was according to any plan I originally laid out. Every other time my life changed, I was fighting to become something and someone I never was. This time the fight was nonexistent. I no longer had to fight for anything, everything was magically falling into place.

I did not care to make anyone else happy right now other than my children, myself, and God, and that is one hell of an empowering feeling. One I had never experienced before. Thinking back to when I was a teenage girl, I could remember getting into an argument with my mother over a piercing I wanted to get. She did not want me to get the piercing because she was concerned about what others would say and think about it.

I remember asking her why should I care what she or anyone else thought when she along with everyone else does not even like who they are? Looking back, that statement still holds a lot of weight to this day. I never cared too much about what other people thought of me and was always thankful for my IDGAF (I do not give a fuck) mentality, but I had a soft spot for my children. I deeply cared about everything they thought and only wanted to do better for them and myself.

I woke up the next morning to a bunch of missed calls and texts. I checked my texts and two of them were from Antonio, three of them from Mack, and the other two from Emanii and King. I began reading the text messages:

(Emanii)
"Hey Mom, I miss you! I need to come back home immediately –
I can't be out here anymore. Please send the cabs!!"

(Me)
"Hi, my beautiful baby girl! I miss you even more! You must
stay with your father. This is the only time he gets with you and he
only gets you guys two months out of the year. Try to hang on. You
do not have much longer to go! I love you very much!! XOXOX"

(King)
"Mom, you need to get us out of here, man! I want to come back
home. It is boring AF here and there is nothing to do. If I check
with him first, is it okay with you if we fly back early?"

(Me)
"Hi my beautiful baby boy! You two need to stop it right now. Two months out of the year is all you must go there for. You both can deal. Love you. Xoxo"

(Mack)
"Good morning, Ms. Wolf. I have prepared the business plan information within a very detailed report and sent that your way a few minutes ago. If you have questions about anything, please let me know. Did you think about coming to the party this evening? I will send the car to come and pick you up at 8:30 pm sharp. Be ready."

(Me)
"Send the car to my home. I will be ready."

(Antonio)
"What up Cam! Call me when you get this. I need to see you. Soon.
Good morning, BTW. Hit me up!"

I then called Antonio and he answered the phone chipper as ever.

"Well, good morning!"

"Good morning, Antonio. Your messages sounded urgent. Is everything okay?"

"Everything is more than okay. I just pulled up to your hotel. I'm outside your room, open the door."

"WHAT?! Are you serious?!!"

"I guess there's only one way to find out."

I ran to the door and opened it. "ANTONIO!!!" I could not believe my eyes!!! I was so excited, and this was exactly what I needed!! He brought bouquet of white roses from behind his back,

"For you," he said with a big grin on his face. "Your eyes!"

"Oh my gosh, come in, come in! I'm so happy to see you, you just don't know! You're starting to make a habit of bringing me white flowers, thank you! How long do I have you? Wait, what brings you here?"

"Business. I have a few things I need to take care of and since I was in the area, I figured I would stop by and see my homie. Besides, you didn't think you were going to this party without me, did you? Ummm...But seriously though, your eyes changed. Are you wearing contacts?"

"I did not even know you knew about the party. Hell, I didn't even know I was going to the party until this morning. I am glad you are here, though. We are gonna have FUN!"

Hoping this time worked in deflecting his question about my eyes. He said,

"Show me to your closet dah-ling. We must coordinate our efforts!"

Thankful the deflecting finally worked, we headed back into my room and went through the clothes that I brought with me to Miami. He ultimately decided that nothing was good enough and that it was time to go shopping. Who was I kidding - I did not go out to parties anymore, I was a mother now and my wardrobe reflected that. I only brought a couple of business suits, shorts, and beach clothes. I was not prepared for a party, especially a party of this caliber.

"Get ready, we are going shopping, my dear! Your closet needs help and I know a perfect place! I also have something a little funky lined up for us to do after you find something you like. We will grab some grub from a place nearby, if you are up for it. Go on now and get ready! Be quick, I am a busy man dah-ling."

Hell, I'm not arguing with that! I hopped in the shower and threw on some blue jean shorts with a fitted white t-shirt. Almost half an hour later, I was finally ready to go.

"Beautiful dah-ling!" Antonio said, clapping his hands together. "Took you long enough, Dag!"

"Hey, if someone would have given advanced notice that they were coming, maybe they would not be sitting here waiting right now. I would have already been ready to go for you."

"But then that would have ruined the element of surprise."

"True story... I appreciate this wonderful surprise. Good thing I get ready quick, if I must say so myself."

"Oh whatever," he said, laughing. "Let's go, slowpoke."

"We never got the chance to talk about all the information you gave me in those boxes."

"Wait – you already went through and read all of that stuff I gave you?"

"Not yet, I got the information at least separated and categorized. I looked at a few of the docs that were in the piles I made and it's some dark, twisted, and sick shit. Have you looked at any of that stuff? Where did it all come from?"

"I will answer every question you have, to the best of my ability, after you have read everything that's in there. It is indeed some very dark stuff. But, there's a reason I gave you that information."

"What the – "

"We have arrived, my dear. Let us find you something special. I cannot have my homie going out in anything less than the best. There will be a ton of pictures taken tonight and I want to make sure you stand out from the rest. Are you ready?" He asked, lowering his sunglasses to look at me.

Laughing at him, I replied, "I was born ready, honey!"

"Okay, dah-ling! Let's get it! I had the girls pull a couple of dresses in advance, which I thought you might like. I know you do not like people picking things out for you, but when I saw these, they absolutely screamed *you*! Besides, if you pick from one of those dresses, I will have the perfect matching outfit!"

When we arrived inside the Versace store, we were greeted by two beautiful women who had two glasses of champagne already poured.

"Welcome to Versace, Ms. Wolf, and Mr. Jasper. We have your requested items prepared for you in a special room in the back.

Please come with us this way. Yasmine will be Ms. Wolf's designer and I will be your designer, Mr. Jasper. I'm Lydia."

They handed us our glasses of champagne and we headed to the back.

"Yasmine, I do not drink. Do you have any water, by chance?" I hated to be the complicated one, but alcohol this early is a big no-no for me. "I'm sure Antonio would more than love that second glass," I said, to reassure them it would not go to waste.

"Oh, no worries at all, Ms. Wolf. Do you prefer Evian or Essentia?"

"Essentia, please."

"Certainly, it's my pleasure. I will be right back with your water." Yasmine said as she left the room to locate the water.

"You just had to be the difficult one, huh?" Antonio said jokingly.

"Jerk."

"Good thing I drink and have no problem drinking yours too. No worries there."

Yasmine returned a few minutes later with a cold and refreshing bottle of Essentia along with a wine glass to pour and drink it from.

"Thank you, Yasmine. I appreciate you!"

"Of course, Ms. Wolf. It's really no problem at all."

"Please call me Cam."

"Certainly, Cam. Are you ready to try on your items? On this rack, I have prepared them for you. If you need anything while you are in there, please let me know. I am happy to help in any way that I can."

"Thank you, Yasmine"

I headed over to the rack, there were three different dresses picked out for me. After trying on all three, I ended up deciding on the third dress, which was perfect! The mini dress was sleeveless and had a bodycon fit. It was black, with an all-over garland design in gold. The racerback had a kind of Miami feel to it. It was perfect for a party; especially a party in Miami where networking would be essential.

"Quite the selection, Ms. Wolf!" Antonio said as he began clapping. "You look nothing short of absolutely amazing! Breath taking, in fact."

"Why thank you, Mr. Jasper," I replied, smiling back.

"You should let that thing out more often, instead of always hiding it away."

I could tell the champagne was kicking in.

"Please – I am a woman who is starting a business in a male-dominated arena. I command respect because I am an excellent businesswoman, not because of my looks. That distinction is key. Besides, if I was wearing stuff like this every day, I would feel inclined to question people's motives. Not to mention, it just brings unnecessary attention I do not want."

"I completely understand. However," he began as he stood to his feet. "Your beauty will naturally attract people and business because both people and business are attracted to beauty itself. So, to me, you are not only an excellent businesswoman but a beautiful one too." He touched my chin and kissed my forehead.

"You do not look too bad yourself, Mr. Jasper! Let me change out of this and we can go."

I went back into the changing room and changed back into the original clothes I came in. By the time I came out of the dressing room, the dress I picked along with Antonio's clothes he picked out had been packaged up for us and was ready to go.

"The next place we're going is somewhere new to me and I'm hoping it's something new for you, too."

"What is this next place? Or is it a surprise?"

"Are you hungry?" He asked, suddenly changing the topic.

"A little."

"I only ask because there's a fancy little Chinese spot right next door to it. I wanted to take you to a fortune teller. Have you ever been to one before?"

"I have not, so I guess this is something new for me. I have always wanted to go to one though. This should be interesting!"

"I could not agree more. Well, looks like we are both in store for something new today. We are about ten minutes away."

We pulled up to a little blue house that had a flashing sign that read, "Fortune Teller Psychic Readings" on the outside. The house was engulfed in green vines that went all along the outside of the home. As we walked up to the entrance, dream catchers and wind chimes were hanging from the patio roof in front of the patio door.

Antonio rang the doorbell. An old lady with messy white hair came to the door. She had rings on every finger and a big jeweled necklace that held a black stone in the center. She had the brightest green eyes that peered through the screen door as she looked out at us.

"Come in, come in," she said. "Follow me to the back."

The house was dark inside, all the curtains were closed. We followed her to the back of the house, into a room where there was a round table with six chairs. There was a black candle in the center of the table with a Ouija board sitting towards the chair nearest to the back. The older lady took a seat in that chair, and we sat on either side of her.

"Are you both here for readings, or just one of you?" She asked, putting her glasses on.

"Both of us," Antonio replied.

The woman then got up and picked up a jar from the window sill.

"Place your donation in here and we will get started."

She handed the jar over to Antonio, where he put some money in. I reached into my purse and pulled out some cash I had and put that in the jar as well.

"Thank you," she said as she placed the jar back on the window sill and walked back over to the table where we were sitting. She looked at me and said,

"Think of a question you would like to know the answer to. It needs to be clear and open-ended. Once you have a question in mind, let me know."

"Can you do his reading first? I need some time to think of a question."

She then looked at him and said the same. Once he had his question in mind, she grabbed a deck of cards and began shuffling them. She then handed them to him and asked him to shuffle them as well. He took the deck of cards and did as she requested. Once he had shuffled the deck twice, she took the deck back and spread the cards out, facing him.

"Pick three," she said.

He chose his three cards; her flipping them over as he chose.

"The upright Emperor, the upright Priestess, and the reversed Queen of Wands," she began,

"The upright emperor says that you are symbolic of the masculine principle itself. You are a father figure to many and provide structure, rules, and a system for people to operate within. You appear to be an upstanding citizen to many and a leader to many more.

"The Upright High Priestess is telling you that you need to listen to your inner voice. Trust your intuition rather than using your normal, more logical, and analytical approach to things. There are questions you seek the answers to. You are becoming more open to your spirituality and will find the answers you seek within.

"The reversed Queen of Wands is saying that either yourself or someone you know needs your help right now. The Queen of Wands is associated with feelings and emotions, the reverse reflecting the negative attributes of these feelings and emotions."

Ending her prophecy, she concluded,

"It would appear the calm demeanor you are often known for keeping may be tested in the days to come. Do not allow your emotions to sway or change your usual practical approach to things. If you give in to your emotions and allow them to lead the way, you will become hated for the things you were once praised for."

She then turned to me and asked me if I had my question ready. Once I told her I was ready, she began the shuffling process again, and I picked my three cards.

"The Upright Ace of Pentacles, The Upright Queen of Swords, and the upright Ace of Wants. My, my, miss lady! I knew there was something about you the moment I laid eyes on you. Big things are in store for you, my dear," she exclaimed,

"The Upright Ace of Pentacles shows you are at a new beginning. A new beginning that will bring an abundance of wealth, health, and prosperity, if watered and cared for properly. This is the time to follow your dreams. The universe is on your side and will see it through for you. New opportunities will be presented to you that will come in various forms, but all will yield exponential results.

"The Upright Queen of Swords is a Queen that does not make emotion-based decisions. Since she is upright, that means you are acting with logic, and you are well respected within your field. Your communication is clear, concise, and frank. Which you expect to be given back to you. This may intimidate others, but it is clear your intellect is sharp and perceptive, and you are determined in your journey.

"The Upright Ace of Wands is here to provide an end to your struggles. You are reaching a point of balance with the progress you have made. You can slowly see the castle coming into view in the distance, which represents the plethora of future opportunities that will knock on your door."

Finalizing her readings, she said,

"Whether you are looking for love, a new career, a change in your finances, or maybe looking for changes with all three, you are about to get them. You are here with a specific purpose or a mission to complete. I also see a glow that surrounds you, like a light.

"Whatever your purpose or mission, you are being protected and guided by this glowing light or higher power. A lot of responsibility will fall upon you in the days ahead, but you know this because you know you are the chosen one."

She then looked at me, smiled, and grabbed my hand.

"I know who you are, my dear, and your secret is safe with me. I can also see what is ahead for you in the days to come. You will lead millions that will look to you for knowledge, inspiration, truth, and hope. But be careful, beautiful yet terrifying one, for not all things are as they appear. Continue to rely on your light – it will illuminate your path and seal you in its protection. It will guide you and protect your path."

Once Antonio and I left the fortune teller he looked and me and asked,

"What was all that about? All that, I know who you are stuff?"

I smiled and shrugged off his question. I knew exactly what she was talking about, but I did not feel like diving into that lengthy conversation. Especially not when we have a party to attend in a matter of a few hours.

"That's a conversation for another day," I replied and looked out the window at the scenery on the drive back home.

"Hopefully one day we can finally have that conversation along with the one about how your eye color changed. I do not know what's going on but just know when you're ready to talk about it or if you ever need to talk about it, I'm here."

I looked over at him and smiled. I could tell Antonio was puzzled by what was going on, but it was better left this way, at least for now. I was never one to believe much in the whole fortune-telling thing, but her reading was eerily accurate. She was able to see who I was and she also knew that I was opening a new chapter in my life.

We pulled up the Chinese restaurant that was nearby and got our food to go. After the reading, we were running close to time to leave for the party. On the ride back to the hotel, I stared out the window, getting lost in thought. This new chapter of my life that I was embarking upon was exhilarating yet terrifying due to all the unknown and uncharted terrain.

We were both quiet for most of the ride back; both of us were taken aback by our readings and partially starved from being out most of the day. As I stared out the window, I couldn't help but wonder what was ahead for me and what else the fortune teller could see that I could not. I closed my eyes and tried to quiet my mind to enjoy the night that was ahead of me.

~ 8 ~

CHAPTER EIGHT:

Phase IV. –Let go

We always want to know what happens at the end – is it a good ending or a bad one? Am I doing everything I can to take me where I need to go? am I evolving in the way I should be evolving? Am I headed in the right direction? Am I a good person or is the sum of my past action's indicators of something else?

The questions tend to pile up, most without answers.

Then, suddenly, you realize, heaven or hell, good or bad; you are who you are and at some point, you must let the logistics go and trust the process.

Wherever that process takes you.

The fog was lifting. I no longer questioned myself countless times in an endless loop about things I should or should not do. It was almost as if this transmutation process was just bringing out my inner self, my real self, my higher self; doing away with the self-doubting, naïve, and lost, prior self. Since the accident, I had turned into quite the homebody and seldomly left the house to do anything.

I cut off all personal relationships and only maintained a close and chosen few. After removing all public information, social media accounts, and all traces of my online existence; I had to get used to being an individual all over again. Thinking back to previous parties I attended, I felt anxious. I could only hope and pray this party would be different.

When I was younger and went to parties, I always felt like the odd one out. I never wanted to be there and only ever went to accompany friends. Parties and their whole atmosphere, were lame to me and in most cases ended terribly. Especially for the sober ones, like myself, who had to endure the drunk stupidity of the ones that could not handle their liquor.

It was usually a complete shit fest! Leaving me to be the mother hen; trying to track down where my friends were, making sure they were not being date raped or worse. Antonio yelled up to me,

"The car is here!"

I was still in my room grabbing the last couple of things I needed to head out.

"Be right there!"

I grabbed my purse and my keys and then sprayed some of my favorite perfume on my wrists and neck. I headed into the main area with Antonio standing in his matching Versace attire. He had a grin on his face and his eyes were looking at me in a way I had not seen before.

"I know I have said this a million times, but you look stunning tonight! I also want to add, that I have impeccable taste! My goodness!"

Both of us laughed and he extended his arm out to me. I put my arm inside his and together we walked out to the truck that was waiting out front for us. I looked at him and said,

"Good choice in outfits, I like the matchy-match-ness we have going on right now! Oh, and you also look stunning tonight, yourself!"

He certainly was one hell of a beautiful man. He was one hell of a man that will make some woman happy one day. As we headed to the party, which was on the downtown South Beach strip, there were scads of people walking all over the streets. Presumably headed to their parties for the night.

Once we got to Collins Avenue (the part of the strip where our party was), the crowd became even denser. Antonio and I looked at each other as if exchanging similar thoughts with one another in anticipation. We arrived at the beautiful and luxurious Setai, where the networking party was being hosted.

The truck pulled us around to the front entrance door. There were bright lights everywhere, and calm tunes played by Kaskade in the background. The melody, wind, scenery, and people created an elusively seductive environment. My intrigue was at an all-time high. The entrance had beautiful trees that lit up everything that was around it.

As we made our way into the hotel, many more trees were going along the edges of the room, sitting in islands of water producing a mirrored effect. Looking around, there had to be at least two to three hundred people here, all on the first floor. Neither of us being fans of large crowds, we made our way to the courtyard area where Mack told us our table would be.

So far, I was pleasantly surprised with this party, it was like nothing I had been to before. The courtyard was equally beautiful as the entrance and the inside, both sceneries equally matched in pure tranquility. As a person operating with high anxiety, especially heightened in large social gathering situations; I deeply appreciated this mellow, low-key feeling environment on many levels.

I took a moment to take the architecture in, making notes of the things I liked and wanted to incorporate into my resort. Once Antonio and I got past all the red tape and made our way back to Mack, he said,

"I am glad you guys finally made it! My, My, Ms. Wolf! You look breathtakingly gorgeous tonight! I am even more pleased you accepted my invitation and came out."

Before I could get a word out, Antonio placed his hand on his hip and said,

"Well, let us not all pretend the world's most handsome bachelor didn't walk in the room and isn't standing right before you! Bow ZE heads! The Elephant King has entered the room!!"

We all burst out in laughter. Antonio sure knew how to break the ice, no matter the situation. This is one of the more prominent attributes that make him the relevant and successful businessman that he is.

"Never a dull moment with you, Antonio. Come this way, I have a few people I want to introduce the both of you to. I have a feeling that you guys are going to hit it off!"

Making our way through the courtyard by the pool seating area, there were a few small groups of people standing around talking. We approached the first group of people who introduced themselves as Mariana, Joel, and Ivan, who were also commercial developers in the Miami area.

These were the heavy hitters in the Florida commercial real estate market. They were responsible for a lot of the new food venues and store markets here in Florida. We spoke with them briefly and made our way to the second group. As we approached the second group of people consisting of one man and two women, I could not help but notice the way the man creepily stared me down the entire time we headed his way.

I felt like I was being sized up for dinner later or some kind of strange ritualistic sacrifice he planned to do later. Once we approached the group, he silenced the women who were talking to him and said to me,

"YOU are someone new here," he took my hand and kissed it softly. "Your beauty is captivating - different from the rest, nothing like I have ever seen before! Tell me, what is it you do? What brings you to Miami? I must know more about you."

Taking my hand back from his rather firm grip, I said,

"I am opening a resort in the area. We just broke ground on the construction a couple of days ago."

"Short and to the point, I like you even more! What is your name?"

"My friends call me Cam. You can call me Ms. Wolf."

Everyone burst into laughter at my sarcastic remark. However, I was not smiling, I was serious. This strange man was creeping me out and I was ready to get the hell out of here, or at least away from him! I tugged at Antonio's arm, letting him know I was ready to go when the strange man then said,

"I'm Clyde and I'm a recruiter."

"... and what is it you recruit for?" I asked him, cringing on the inside as I waited for his response.

"Beauty and talent; which you appear to possess both. You are fierce and you know it, honey! It is written all over you, especially in that stride. You need to share your beauty with the world! Here, please, take one of my cards."

The card read "Clyde Mitchell, SVP Recruitment, Wilhelmina Models, New York, NY." His address, email, and phone numbers were also listed on the card. I was not interested in modeling. Never have been, never will be.

"Thank you," I said, not knowing what else to say.

"If I do not hear from you, I will track you down and find you myself, Ms. Wolf. Even if only for one photoshoot. This is non-negotiable - I have many plans for you, Ms. Wolf! Many plans!"

Walking away, I had a gut feeling this would not be my last encounter with this creepy little man. Mack, Antonio, and I headed over to the third group of people. Halfway there, I stopped Mack about halfway in his stride and said,

"Warn me now if you are taking me to meet another complete nut within this next group."

Both Mack and Antonio burst out in laughter. I did not find it funny in the slightest. It was totally cringe-worthy, and I had never met such an odd character in my entire life. Once Mack and Antonio stopped laughing, Mack looked at me and said,

"The next group of people you will be meeting are much milder. They are very knowledgeable, and they requested to meet you directly tonight."

"Why?" I immediately asked.

"You are funny Ms. Wolf. I know you believe you keep a low profile, but the moment you began construction building a multi-million-dollar resort, you became top of the list to meet for many people. Come, you will see."

We made our way over to the next group of individuals; this group was slightly larger, with five men and three women. They were major medical marijuana growers and distributors here in Florida and I liked the way they thought. They looked at the bigger picture and were making plans to expand up the east coast as marijuana was becoming more widely accepted and legalized nationally. Out of curiosity, I asked the group,

"I am told an introduction was requested. How did you come to find out who I am?"

Kelly, one of the distributors, replied,

"I know everything, Ms. Wolf, everything that has value anyway. I believe that the resort you are opening provides a lot of value, which will, in turn, provide a lot of lucrative opportunities to many kinds of suppliers and consumers. We want to be on your radar for suppliers. I believe we can be of mutual benefit to each other in many ways and in a lot of different areas."

"I couldn't agree more," I responded as I reached into my purse to pull out a business card. "Here is my business card. We will get a meeting set up to discuss some ideas."

We exchanged contact information and one of the growers named Dwayne said,

"Thank you for taking the time out this evening to meet with us. We look forward to speaking with you."

We made our way around the room with Mack introducing us to several groups of people; literary agents, influencers, videogra- phers, photographers, techies, and a plethora of smaller business owners, in the Miami area. The guests at this party enamored me offering an eclectic mix of networking results. This was the first party that I had been to since transitioning into this new me, and so far, there was nothing I didn't like.

I appeared to attract all the right people, places, and things at precisely the right time in my life. Life was no longer happening *to* me; it was happening *for* me! Several hours later, we finally made our way to our empty table. We were supposed to be here a while ago and the five-inch stilettos I wore that night were killing my feet! As I sat down, I could feel almost immediate relief. My mother used to say, "Beauty is pain" and this is one thing I could agree with her about right now.

This is also why I prefer a pair of joggers, a t-shirt, and some Nikes with my hair up in a bun. I was not this well-put-together person people believed I was. Most days, I was an absolute mess. I hardly ever wore makeup. When I would wear makeup, it was never anything more than mascara and eyeshadow, and for the days I was feeling a little frisky, I would put on a little eyeliner too, but that was the extent of it.

Anything more than that was just doing way too much, not to mention nothing I ever had the patience for. I did not understand how some women had time to put entire masks of makeup on in the morning. When I was over here doing well just to wake up on time. Antonio grabbed my hand, squeezed it, and said,

"You look exhausted. Want to get out of here?"

Mack interjecting,

"You guys are getting old. It is only a little past one in the morning. Can't you can hang out longer? We have a little buffet going over there. Help yourselves."

I was exhausted and nothing at the buffet looked even remotely appetizing. I looked back at Mack and said,

"Tonight, was amazing and I am so glad we came out. I am also thankful for the new connections, but I need to get home and rest my feet amongst other things."

"I just - "

Before he could get another word out, I stopped him and said,

"Mack please give this ticket to the valet for us. I will be headed downstairs in about five minutes."

Antonio then took the ticket and handed it to him and said,

"The lady means business."

With that, Mack made his way down the stairs to the valet area.

"Thanks, Antonio," I said. "You don't have to leave with me, I can send the truck back for you once he drops me off. That way, it will give you more time to network a bit more and 'do your thing' with the ladies."

"I am not here for that. I am here for you, and other business that I'll attend to tomorrow. I am ready to go when you are."

We went downstairs to the valet area where Mack was waiting by our truck.

"I hope you two had fun and made some worthy connections while you were here," Mack said. "More is coming, Ms. Wolf. Keep your phone by you. Something is telling me that in the days ahead, you and I will be quite busy." He had a smile on his face that went from ear to ear.

Antonio shook his hand and said,

"I had a great night and believe it was a success. Until next time."

"Have a wonderful evening, Ms. Wolf, and Mr. Jasper. Talk soon."

The entire way back home, Antonio picked with me about the strange model agent guy from the party. He kept trying to change my perception to see how that interaction could lead to something fruitful versus something antagonizing. I did not enjoy being stared at like a piece of meat and I couldn't see that changing.

"It is good to know your idea and work are being supported by the community. This support is usually measured at the opening and we can somewhat gauge by the results of tonight. This indicates to me that the actual opening will be nothing short of complete success!

"The owner of this future resort has a passion that paints a color the world has never seen before. This color brings things out of people they didn't even know existed. You have always had this gift. It is like you can make any old thing new again, by giving it new life. Kind of like what you have done for me."

"What do you mean?"

"I mean you brought me back, Cam. Look - before you came back into my life, things were dull and meaningless. I went through the daily motions not questioning anything other than things on business reports. My conversations and relationships are business and family-related.

"Nothing past the surface level. Women I meet are usually only interested in one thing - money. This keeps me to myself and to the people I knew before I started this business. I can honestly tell you, I have not had a meaningful conversation with anyone in years. Not like the conversations we have. This adventure with you has been refreshing. Even if just for this moment, I am glad you came back into my life."

"You are saying this stuff like I am going somewhere. I am not going anywhere. Besides, I could not get rid of you even if I wanted to."

Antonio began laughing and said,

"You are like a storm on a warm night in Miami. You provide the perfect environment for partying all night in the warm sweet air of the night. Then, when you least expect it – BAM! You bring the storm; a torrential downpour with echoing thunder and radiating lightning. Only leaving traces of where you have been behind in the morning sun.

"What I have learned about you is that you never stay in one place for too long and try your best to refrain from long-term relationships as well. You have maintained about two relationships since high school with one of those relationships ending in divorce. I do not know everything there is to know about you, but what I do know is there is something about you that everyone falls in love with. You are going places in life and will lead and inspire many people."

Within the past five years, I had lived in four different states and knew several people but no longer had contact with any of them. There was no point. I did not have much of anything in common with them anymore and as Antonio also mentioned, I didn't have any friends I considered real friends. Friends that penetrated through the surface-level layer of bullshit.

He was right and I could admit since the accident happened, things had gotten way worse in the socializing department of my life. No one ever really said the things they meant or meant the things they said, most being too afraid to just be themselves due to internal insecurities. I did not like having to walk on eggshells when I spoke to people, least of all to people I consider a friend and that wouldn't start now.

"Well, we are here. I will walk you to the door."

"Wait – you're not staying the night with me?"

"I will have to leave in a couple of hours for a meeting and after, I have to fly back west coast to take care of more business. I did not want to wake you with me having to leave early."

"I know you are a busy man and I also appreciate these moments together however brief they are. We can put on some Netflix and chill until we fall asleep or until you must go to your meeting, whichever happens first."

Accepting my offer, we headed inside the suite I was staying at while in Miami. He went straight over to the refrigerator to hunt for food, and I went to the back and changed into some shorts and a t-shirt. I then made my way back out to the main area. The room was a bit cool, so I turned the air off and opened the balcony doors to allow the warm breeze in. I grabbed some blankets and pillows from my things in the back and prepped our chill area for us to lie in. Antonio returning from the kitchen area looked over to me and said,

"I made us two blasts from the past!"

He was carrying two plates of peanut butter and jelly sandwiches with cut-up apple and kiwi slices.

"Oh, my gosh! I remember this!! Your mom always used to make this for you and pack it for your lunch, then you would always share half of it with me at school. I think she eventually caught on because she started packing you two of everything, remember?" I began laughing when thinking back to this.

"She thought I was just a growing boy," he said, also laughing. I think sometimes she knew and just didn't want to say anything, so she'd just pack two." His laughing came to a sudden stop.

"I kind of feel bad about that now, for not just telling her, you know? But I did not want to make things worse for you and your brothers. You love your brothers so much, and I knew that a lot of the suffering you were going through must have been for them. So, I never wanted to be that one to cross that line with you. Although I will admit, there were many nights I felt torn about what to do."

"Sorry I put you through that, I really am. But I am also very thankful for you because if it wasn't for you, I wouldn't have had a lot of things. Including this new future right now that is all because of you."

His serious face went away, and he began laughing again and said,

"You would have had this new future, regardless. If not me, it would have been someone else. I was just the first and only one you pitched to. It is that light you have inside of you, Cam. That light attracts all kinds of people, good and bad. You cannot help who the light will attract; similar to lights at night, but you can use that light to attract what you want and need. You will, in time, get better at keeping away the ones you do not want to get close."

I am not sure why, but something came over me and I felt an urge inside of me to reach up and kiss him. His lips looked so moist from the juices in the fruits and the more he licked them, the more I felt inclined to act. I fought the urge and reminded myself of my number one rule; do not shit where you eat.

As I kept fighting this flaming urge, I could feel a heat sensation heat my entire body, like something was heating it from the inside. I suddenly felt a trickle of sweat drip onto my t-shirt from my underarms. *Oh no,* I thought, *where the hell is this coming from?!* I did not understand where this was suddenly coming from.

I was around him all the time, especially lately, and never had such thoughts like this. I had not felt this way about anyone in a very long time and did not want anything to come between our friendship more than anything else. In my past, I was prone to act based on feelings.

This time, I decided to listen to my head; refusing to do anything that would or could even potentially derail or detrimentally impact our rekindled friendship. I was standing on new ground, in new territory and I wasn't quite sure how to navigate out of this one. Antonio, raising his eyebrows, looked at me and asked,

"Are you okay?"

"Yeah, I am. Hang on, I am going to run to the bathroom really quick and take a cool shower. I will be right back." I replied.

Antonio looking instantly confused, I hopped up and headed to the bathroom. My body had turned into a complete heat box. I needed cool water, and I needed it now! I stripped off my clothes, turned on the shower water, and hopped in. I stood there for a minute thinking about the conflict between my mind and my body, trying to make sense of it.

Even though I could not make much logical sense of what was going on inside of me, what I did know was that I wasn't at a time in my life when I was ready to commit again. It had been several years since I had divorced. I have met several people, but none of them were able to hold my interest any longer than a few weeks at a time. I did not want Antonio being sucked into this cycle, or my whimsical, at times, nature.

He was a phenomenal man, one of a kind, and he deserved a better woman than the woman I could offer him right now. As I turned off the water to the shower and could see a figure through the glass doors. I went to open the shower door when my towel was flung over the glass doors by the figure that was once in the distance.

"I know why you came back to shower," he said.

The heat came back into my body. I did not know why he was in here or what he came in to do, but my body seemed to be aware.

"Why do you think I came back to shower?"

"Because there is a connection between us, Cam. A connection we have never explored before. We are humans that are attracted to each other; you're beautiful and you know I'm beautiful. I think it is completely normal to react in such conditions. Remember when you were at my place when we were talking and I suddenly got up and started pacing?"

"Yes, I remember."

"Well, that was my way of getting my mind in check because I could see that feeling wasn't mutual. But tonight, something changed on your side and I could feel that too. Something I have been waiting for, for a very long time. Then you take off and hide from me. It's like you have never once considered me more than a friend, until now, right here at this specific moment. There is something I need to know, something that I must know; why can't I have you? Why aren't I good enough for you?"

My heart dropped; he is taking everything the wrong way! This is not how this was supposed to go, I needed to make this right. I dried myself off, wrapped my towel around me, and came out of the shower, now facing him.

"Antonio you are an amazing man! How could you ever doubt this?! Why do you instantly think you are not good enough for me? You are completely off base. We are business partners now. I do not shit where I eat and, more than anything, I don't want anything to come between our friendship."

"We are so much more than that and you know it! You take these new moments in time and erase all our history with them. I see who you are, even when you try to hide. I see where you are going and know where you've been and yet, even so, here I am, standing in front of you, being rejected for the millionth time. As if you do not see me the same way I see you, even when your body physically tells us both so."

With that he stormed out of the bathroom and went back into the main area. Thinking about what he said, he was right. We were so much more than that. I also wanted to cross that line and explore, but now just was not the time for that. I did not want this good thing we have right now ruined. He was worth so much more than I could offer right now and me giving myself to him would only pacify our emotions at this moment.

In the grand scheme of things, this would do nothing for either of us other than create chaos. There were still a lot of things I needed to figure out, and I could not afford any distractions right now. My track history proved I was incapable of committing to people long term. Regardless of what he thought or believed, I refused to drag him into my madness. Whether or not he could see it, he deserved better.

I found some clothes and dressed. I headed back out to the main living area where Antonio was laying down looking through stuff to watch on Netflix. I went over and sat down next to him, looking him in his eyes, and said,

"Antonio, you deserve the world, the stars, everything around it, below it, and above. I am not at a point in my life where I can offer you even a fourth of that. I also cannot afford any distractions right now. You are used to this roller coaster life and have used it to find yourself and make a name for yourself. I need you to allow me to do the same.

"If we are meant to be we will remain or find our way back to each other when the time is right for us both, not just for one. I have known you for over half my life and nothing can change that or take that away, nor do I want it to. We made our way back to each other for a reason and I am here to stay. If you will let me?"

His glossy eyes just stared at me. I could tell there was so much he wanted to say but he was choosing not to. He looked at the TV and then said,

"Even as much as this kills me, I respect your wishes, as I always have, 'cause I am a good guy and all. I love you, Cam, whether you like it or not. Trust me, sometimes I wish I could turn these feelings I have for you off, even back in high school, but I just can't. You are my best friend and I honestly can't see life without you in it again, and we've only reconnected a few months ago. I like this connection we have, but it scares me sometimes because I know tomorrow is not promised to either of us.

"Your accident serves as a daily reminder to me and I'm sure of you, too. I do not want to lose you again and I do not want to push you away, either. With that being said, I will wait for you. I do not care how long it takes. When you are ready, I promise, I will show you what genuine and unconditional real love is. Love you do not have to question, love that shows up every day and never gives up. The love you have never experienced before that fills your entire soul with knowledge and guidance to grow, do and become better, the love *you* deserve.

"Until that time comes, I will always be here. I am not going anywhere, even if you are frustrating sometimes. I will think of new ways to woo you when I wake up."

A smile finally appeared on his face. He took my hand and led us into the bedroom area. He pulled back the covers to the bed for me to get in and then he hopped in next to me. I did not know what I did to deserve such a beautiful man, inside and out, but I decided Antonio would be the only man I would have eyes for going forward.

This amount of loyalty, persistence, and commitment is something that could never be bought, bargained for, or won. It was something he simply gave freely. He was the man of my dreams, the king I had always longed for, and finally, he had arrived and was willing to wait. I felt like the luckiest woman in the world.

He turned me over and kissed me on my forehead, nose, both cheeks, and then a nice and slow kiss on my lips. His lips were warm, soft, and gentle, smelling of his Jean Paul cologne he put on for the party we just attended.

"Good night, beautiful." He said before laying his head down on the pillow next to me, pulling me close to him.

"Good night, beautiful man," I replied.

We fell asleep holding each other that night, with me in his arms. I find a nice little nook right in between his chin and shoulder within the neck area, and fell asleep to the sound of our hearts becoming synchronized.

*****

As I dozed off in this blissful synchronized harmony I found myself in, I was brought to the lake and could see Pooh off in the distance. She was skipping her way toward me. It has been so long since I have seen her! I was so happy to see her again!

"Hey, Pooh! It has been forever!!" We hugged at first sight.

"It took you a while to find your way out of the wilderness, but you found the light and now you can see! You have made us proud! You finally figured out you must trust the process. I know it has been hard for you to come out of your shell, but it was necessary for you to achieve what's been tasked ahead of you.

"You will receive further instructions in the days ahead from another visitor. This visitor is someone you know very well; although it may take you a moment to remember him. Allow the memories you receive along with the information coming to you in the days ahead to serve as a beacon for interpreting the new information you will soon gain. It would be remiss of me not to pass that information on, as it is of high importance you remember all facets of who you are.

"Hold tight to that in the days ahead, even if you find yourself questioning things. Some information is still being intentionally withheld from you. The reason for this is simple and will be understood at a later point in time. I say to you again, Cam, do not be scared.

"You are always watched over, backed, and guided by a higher power. You are the chosen one, the enlightened one. Additional cerebral networks have been added to the biology of your brain. It will help you understand what you are seeing from the other dimensions and teach you how to interpret this information. It will also create more transformations that will come with the next stage of the activation process, that will be physically noticeable to your outward appearance."

"What about the wolf - I have not seen her since she told me I would go into the abyss. Where did she go?"

"Have you not noticed the change in your eyes, Cam? You and the wolf are one, hence the transformations. The only way you two can separate is through death, and, as you know, energy cannot die, it can only be transmuted. As above, so below; as inside, so outside.

"Remember this in the days ahead and nothing can ever be lost to you. Continue keeping a clear head in the days to come. This clarity will bring great insight into many things to come."

With that, Pooh vanished. I walked over to the lake as I usually did, sat down, and slipped my feet into the water. This rejuvenation never got old and I always made the most of it with every visit. Suddenly, I could see someone in the distance making their way over to me. As this person moved closer, I could see it was the same familiar face I had seen that day while I was in the shower; the dark-skinned man with crystal clear blue eyes.

He stopped once he reached the opposite side of the lake with no words spoken. While he spoke no words, I could feel he wanted to tell me something. We continued exchanging long gazes as if in recognition of one another, but he still did not speak. I decided to get up and walk over to him but as soon as I take my feet out of the water, he disappeared.

*****

$$\sim 9 \sim$$

CHAPTER NINE:

Phase V – Activation

There comes a moment in every person's life when they start to not only question who they are, where they have been, and where they want to go, but also what they are.

By questioning the 'what,' you are opening pandora's box.

You will find the possibilities to be strikingly like that of pure life energy, the most important thing about pure life energy is the fact that it can never die.

Therefore, making **you** immortal.

I woke up after ten that morning to a note from Antonio that read:

"Good morning, beautiful,

I did not have the heart to wake you but am thankful you allowed me to stay with you last night. Just like that one, I can only pray and have faith for more. There is a gift for you on the kitchen counter. Talk soon,
'Toni
XOXOXO"

I walked over to the kitchen table and saw two Versace bags sitting there. I looked inside the bags and found the other two Versace dresses I tried on for the party the other day. He had somehow purchased the other two dresses I had tried on and snuck them in here without me seeing. I could not help but laugh at his tactics, persistence being his strongest characteristic.

I admired a man that knows what he wants and will do whatever it takes to get it. But I also admired the hard-working, loyal, and integral man above all else. While Antonio and I have history, we still had much to learn about who and what we had become over the time we spent apart. The years we spent a part went into the making of who we are now; no longer being two kids in high school with no real-life responsibilities.

I thought back to what had happened the night before with Antonio. I looked over at the Versace bags and could not help but smile. I always dreamed of meeting a man just like this one day and that proverbial one day has finally come. I felt like the luckiest woman in the world, finally living the life of my dreams.

If I would have known all of this would have happened the moment I quit my job at the bank, I would have done it sooner. Looking at my phone, I noticed there were many missed calls and messages. I decided I would shower and mentally digest everything to get myself in gear for the day. Once I was out of the shower, I began reading my messages, emails, and preparing to return missed calls.

When suddenly, my phone rings. I did not recognize the phone number; however, my caller ID was showing the name of Clyde Mitchell. I started thinking to myself, *who did I know named Clyde Mitchell?* Then a flashback to last night's networking came to mind when I remembered the strange model agent guy's name was Clyde Mitchell. I wondered how in the world he found me and got my phone number?! Ugh!! *What could he possibly want?! I told him I was not interested in modeling or becoming one of his latest candidates to parade around in the latest tutu!*

Not being in the mood for a pointless convo, I sent his call to voicemail. However, a few of moments later, a text came through from Mr. Mitchell saying,

"You cannot ignore me, girl! I told you I would find you! I need you downtown in two hours. I told you they would love you, honey! Call me yesterday!"

Ugh... I thought, *I guess I should call him back to see what he is talking about. I don't appreciate him assuming it's okay to just volunteer my time without first consulting with me!* This was all happening so fast, and I was not even sure if this was something I wanted to do. However, I knew I was a full fledge businesswoman now, and exposure was something I needed for my resort. I had to get my face and my name out there, even though I cringed on the inside about putting myself out there.

I have never been a fan of being on display. I have always appreciated anonymity and privacy for many reasons. I did not like the idea of my life being a constant public spectacle and I didn't want my children to go through unnecessary life changes because of the loss of privacy and anonymity. I wanted them to have normal lives with normal life experiences. However, this new me required new thinking.

With being leveled up, I had to be different and act different, to get different results. If I continued the same path, I was only limiting my success. Since that did not sit right with me either, I pursued the ladder and called Mr. Mitchell back.

"Well, Helloo Ms. Wolf! I see you got my messages. I told you I would find you!"

"Yes, I got them. Tell me more about this meeting downtown."

"Honey, I have one of our top clients flying in from New York to meet you. Trust me, you will be thrilled. I know little about you, but what I do know is you have excellent taste and you are very picky. This client is just like you. I sent them a photo of you from the party and they will not have it any other way, honey!

"They want YOU! I am sure this goes without saying, but this will be top dollar client. I understand your time is precious and do not want to waste it. I can assure you; that this meeting will come with many benefits that you will appreciate both professionally and personally. How soon can you be here?"

"Send me the details and I will be there in two hours."

"Wonderful, honey. Details are on the way!"

A few hours later, I met up with Mr. Mitchell at the same place we met at the party, the Setai. I pulled up and gave the valet my key and was given a ticket in exchange. I was walked in and immediately greeted by a resort attendant who took me back to a private business meeting room where Mr. Mitchell was already there with a couple of other people I had never met before.

I was introduced to the other people in the room and was told we were just waiting for this top client of theirs to arrive and would then get things started. Small talk was exchanged for a few minutes until a few moments later when a tall older woman walked into the room with an entourage of her own. Mr. Mitchell and his entourage rose from their seats with smiles ear to ear to greet her and her people.

"Ms. Versace, thank you so much for joining us! We are happy you could make it."

Completely ignoring Mr. Mitchell's greeting, she walked directly to me and said,

"So, this is her? Stand up, darling."

"In the flesh," I responded, standing to my feet. I gave a slow twirl to give her a 360 view of what she came to see. She walked over to an open chair and sat down. I sat back down also anxious for what was next.

"I told you she was amazing," Mr. Mitchell happily interjected.

"Do you have any makeup on?" She asked me, taking a cigarette out of her purse.

"No, not my thing," I replied.

"You are gorgeous! Your beauty is refreshing and reminds me of the old, yet classic Miami. It is youthful, elegant, pure, and I must say very carnivorous. I can also see that you have a duality about yourself. While you look completely innocent and refreshing; you also look like you can be deadly, in many ways." She erupted in laughter.

"I want you to be the face of Versace. You possess the exact look we need to represent this new season's catalog. We would be honored to have you and welcome you into the family. I will send you the terms and details. If you accept, this will be a very lucrative contract. I take care of all my girls as if they were my own."

"Wow... I am honored."

"I told you, honey! You got what we want! I will get you those details." Mr. Mitchell interjected.

"No – you, Clyde, will send her nothing! Leave us and I will discuss it with you later once we are done!" She commanded.

The room was abruptly silenced by her command. Everyone from Mr. Mitchell's team then proceeded to get up and exit the room. Once we had the room to ourselves, she walked over and sat in a chair closer to me and said,

"I want you to know I chose you for a specific reason; a reason other than your looks. You remind me of someone, someone I knew long ago. This may sound crazy to you, but the moment I saw your picture, I had something like a soul recognition of one's soul to another. This recognition gives me a feeling I have not felt in quite a while. Since walking into this room and being in your company, I feel inspired. Inspired to create something new."

"It does not sound crazy at all. I understand exactly what you mean. I have been experiencing a lot of that myself lately. What is even more interesting is the fact that I've never been one to wear brand-name items, but I've always had a soft spot for Versace. Versace is the only brand name I wear if I buy a brand at all. Maybe that was something speaking to my soul way before I ever met you, considering there are no coincidences. We are here in this specific moment for a reason, and I am curious to see where this goes."

She smiled and said,

"I like you. You get me. I am *very* curious about you. Yes, let us see where this goes! You have your attorney review the information I send with you and if anything comes up, call me directly. I wrote my personal cell number on the back."

She took a business card out of her purse and handed it to me.

"Also, I told you, I take care of my girls as if they were my own. You are opening a resort here, yes?"

"Yes," I replied.

"Well, then you will have no have time for Clyde. He will work you into the ground, leaving you no time to oversee your resort. There are not a lot of us women in this business, so we have to stick together and look out for each other. I want to see you finish your resort before committing to such a huge lifestyle change because that is exactly what that would look like. Just think about it, read things over, and get back to me."

Later that evening, I called Emanii, King, Antonio, and Jenayah and told them about my latest meeting with Ms. Versace. They were all elated with excitement for me. Both King and Emanii were still begging me to come back home. They missed their animals, their friends, and of course, they missed their mama. I missed them even more, more than they could possibly understand.

By the time they would return home, everything would be different once again. I looked over the Versace contract sent to my email. Everything looked in line from what I could tell and was very lucrative indeed. I sent it over to my lawyer to have him look at it to make sure everything was copasetic, knowing it would probably be a day or two before he got back to me.

I sent Ms. Versace an email back, letting her know I had received the contract and sent it to my lawyer for review. I let her know I would reach back out and contact her with an update once I have one. Feeling the exhaustion from the day take over, I headed to bed and fell asleep in no time.

*****

In an instant, I was brought back to the magical lake of life. This time the sun was much more radiant than I remembered before. I scanned the scene and noticed the man with blue eyes standing in the distance, staring directly at me. There was something different about his visit this time. I could feel it in the energy in the air. His prowl and demeanor had changed from the other times I saw him.

Hoping for interaction this time, I began walking slowly in his direction, taking in his appearance. He stood at least ten feet tall and was wearing a white robe with a gold sash tied around it. He carried with him a gold ankh, what appeared to be a purse that was in the shape of a triangle, and a goldenrod staff with two snakes intertwined; one white snake, and one black snake that was moving upward upon his staff. The top of the rod had a pair of wings attached to it that shimmered brightly against the lake.

He wore golden shoes that also had a pair of wings attached to them. The glistening of the snakes' scales induced something of a halogenic effect that allured and mystified me. They were drawing me closer to him and with being unable to resist the allure, I continued making my way towards him, quickening my haste.

The beautiful and familiar man still had not spoken a word. I also remained silent, not sure of what this visit would entail, and waited for him to lead the way. He put out his hand to me, and I placed my hand in his. We began making our way towards the lake. He never took his eyes off me and I never took my eyes off him. He put one of his feet over the lake and I followed his leading, putting one of mine over the lake also.

He then pulled me into the lake with him, submerging us both into the magical water. The water took us under and within seconds we arrived at a familiar place I was taken to before. I began recalling where I knew this place from and remembered Pooh brought me here in one of the dreams I had, and she called it 'home.' Whenever I was brought back to this place, it brought back feelings of nostalgia. I just could not place exact memories, timeframes, and people associated with it, but was more than aware that I had a history with this place.

We headed back into the same area as before that had led to the Royal Throne. I did not know who this man was, but whenever I was near him; I felt at home. I felt as though I had known him my entire life, like he had come to me many times, in various forms, throughout my life. He moved with power, grace, and precision, and with rapid speed that was quicker than thought itself.

Once we were right outside the royal throne doors, he took my other hand in his hand. Although towered over me, I was not scared of him or his size. I somehow knew I was in safe hands with him and had nothing to worry about.

"My beloved Heavenly Mother, I know you do not remember me right now, but you will. When you do, you will understand and remember everything else. You have successfully transitioned through your stages of activation and may now proceed into the Royal Throne," he said.

He knelt and leaned forward, gently kissing my forehead. He let go of my hand, bowed his head, gesturing goodbye, and got up and began walking in the opposite direction down the hall. I turned around, facing the Royal Throne's doors. At once, the doors that were once closed flew open as if they had been awaiting my arrival all along. I walked ahead slowly, through the doors.

The room was completely engulfed in the brightest of white light that filled the entire room. The ceiling was swirling with clouds. Big angels flying were flying in and out of the clouds, as if playing peek-a-boo. The room had dense fog that filled the air, making it hard to see directly in front of me. As I would walk forward, the angels would move about in a directing manner. I continued walking forward, looking up, letting the angels on the ceiling be my guide to where I needed to go.

Once I got to the center of the room, I could feel a cool sensation come over me. It was almost as if someone had dropped the temperature drastically within a matter of nanoseconds. I looked around but nothing was in sight through the dense fog. I had no idea of what was happening or who was there, but I could sense someone or something was near me. Growing more anxious, I reached out my hand to feel around but nothing was within reach.

Growing impatient with the Blue's Clues games being played, I asked, "Who's there?"

A figure began emerging from the fog.

"Who are you?" I asked, confused at what I was supposed to be looking at.

The figure came closer, almost within reach, but the fog was too dense to make out any clear features.

"I want to tell you a story about a frog named Glenn." A ruminating and deep voice said to me.

"A frog...really? You brought here to tell me about a frog?" I asked, still unable to make out the details of this figure.

"Yes, really. A lot can be learned from frogs, especially Glenn. Are you unaware of the lifeforce inside of all things, including frogs?"

"I guess so...But, at this point, I am hesitant about them along with any every other reptile. They don't have a good reputation, to be put it nicely. Their gross, slimy, and cannot be trusted."

"Now THAT'S intriguing," the voice said. The voice becoming more masculine, deeper, and there was now a hissing sound to its words like it had a snake tongue itself. The voice was commanding, and it commanded the entire room, including the angels moving about on the ceiling. They froze and stopped moving around the ceiling at her clear offense.

"Why is that?" I hesitantly asked.

"That is a story for another time. Maybe you will be able to piece it together yourself. The story I want to tell you about right now is about Glenn, Glenn the frog. Glenn was a wonderful little tadpole. He always listened to everything his mother and father told him. He always used good wisdom and exercised good judgment, but as Glenn got older becoming an adult frog, he got very lazy and started taking shortcuts.

"His parents always warned him of taking shortcuts and being lazy. However, as Glenn got older, he disposed of his parent's warnings, which were created to steer clear of humans. Glenn thought he knew better than his parent's and their rules were nonsensical. To him, those rules created extra work and Glenn became resentful of this extra work.

"One day, while Glenn was taking his shortcut a little boy named Chris found him. Chris decided he wanted to take Glenn home and keep him as his pet. Glenn did not like this idea too much, but there was nothing he could do. He had been captured by Chris and had no way to communicate with Chris to tell him he did not want to go back to his home.

"Once Chris got back to his house with Glenn, Chris began preparing a nice little cage to put Glenn in to make his home. Glenn saw an open chance and figured he would make a break for it. Glenn hopped right off the desk Chris briefly sat him on while preparing his cage for him and took off as fast as he could! Glenn thought he found a perfect spot to hide, which was inside a very deep pot that was inside of the cabinet. A few hours later, Glenn fell asleep in that deep pot exhausted from his capture.

"Several hours later, Chris's mother was not paying attention and began filling the pot with water to prepare that evening's dinner. Once she had enough water in the pot, she placed it on the stove, turned it on and began boiling the water. She was preparing the water for a chicken she wanted to boil for some nice, hearty, and thick homemade chicken noodle soup. It was her family's favorite recipe!

"Now, Glenn not knowing any better, assumed the water was just hospitality being shown by his new companion, Chris. Glenn continued laying there, bathing in the water, and loving every moment. The water was so warm, becoming even warmer, putting Glenn to sleep. That was until Glenn was instantly woken up by an immense amount of heat that was now coming from the water. The nice, warm water Chris's mother started for the chicken she was planning to boil, was now a rolling boil.

"Glenn tried his hardest to get out of the pot, but he could not seem to muster up enough energy to get himself out. Before you know it, it was too late. Chris's mother never noticed Glenn was in the pot, and added the chicken into the water, covering Glenn in the process. Glenn was boiled along with the chicken that night for dinner. So many lessons can be learned from Glenn and his refusal to listen to the instructions given to him by his parents. His laziness and shortcuts cost him his life."

I stood there in complete silence, not knowing what to do or say next. I did not know what any of this meant, so I just said the first thing that came to my head:

"I did not ask to be here. I was brought here. I am not sure what relevance the story of Glenn has to me. I have not taken any short-cuts nor disregarded any of the instructions I have been given."

"You were given some information. Information you were warned had a price. The price for this information is what brought you here. The price for this information has landed you in that same proverbial pot right now, with me. Will you continue to stay, with this constant pressure to become the diamond you are meant to be? Or will you flee at the first sight of danger?

"Fleeing comes with its own set of consequences. You were warned from the very beginning that all information has a price. A price that must be paid. On the contrary to Glenn's story, this boiling pot will not turn you into chicken soup, it will transform you into who and what you are meant to be. Whether or not you become like Glenn, is up to you."

"Okay, I follow. I'm listening."

"Good. Listen well. That story I told you about Glenn is pivotal to your success. Like Glenn, you are now doing everything right. You do as you are told and follow instructions accordingly. You do not deviate from the path as Glenn did, but that's why Glenn's story is important for you to remember in the days ahead.

"Do not get too comfortable like Glenn did, where you currently are at. It is when you are distracted by the contentment of your surroundings, when they will attack you. As you have been told, there is a lot of information that is being withheld, for many good reasons. You are someone most will find unfathomable and even terrifying at the sight. You, my dear, are a complex organism. One that required careful and thoughtful deliberation. One that is held in high regard with the divine Universal Mind that created you.

"Something you humans have come to term as, 'miracle,' 'savior,' 'angel,' amongst other terms, and that you are. You are a miracle of the cosmos; energy of pure creation. You are a savior to many, especially to all lifeforces. You are an angel to humanity, dedicating yourself to the light and lifeforce within us all. If you knew the truth of who you are, you would have relied upon that instead of finding your own way in the past; creating who you used to be. However, if you truly knew the truth of who and what you are, that would have defeated the ultimate purpose of this plan."

"This plan?" I asked, in confusion.

"Yes, the ultimate plan that was weaved into your story and the story of all Indygos."

"My story? The story of all Indygos?"

"Yes. *Your* story and their story."

"Wait a minute – so this was all written in advance?"

"Yes."

"So, you know how this is going to play out?"

"Yes. I know how everything will play out and everything that plays out is all a part of the ultimate plan created by the divine Universal Mind."

"Who are you?" I asked, still unable to make out the details of this figure.

"You know who I am - you just do not know, that you know, who I am. Prepare yourself. I am going to take you on a trip. A trip back into time; the beginning of time where you and I begin."

~ 10 ~

CHAPTER TEN:

The Royal Orders

Blueprints are the structure that make up our entire lives and
all the contents within it.

These blueprints were engineered by the divine Universal Subconscious Mind. A thoughtful design to all your life experiences.
Something created and decided as a pre-principal to our births.

Something you cannot navigate, deviate from, control or at
times, see.

These blueprints create who you are now, who you will become,
and everything you are meant to be.

I was taken to a place that looked like a luxurious resort in an elegant setting somewhere that looked like Greece. This place was in the middle of a heavily dense rainforest. There were beautiful waterfalls that housed rainbows that echoed all over the enriched land. Tall, luscious trees stood that were composed of cool and vibrant colors, so many new colors I had never seen.

A beautiful island was hidden within their center of this place; only able to be seen as beams of light from the sky would shine through the leaves of this heavily dense rainforest. The island was made up of only women, whose sole duties were to protect the purity and sanctity of the women there both young and old. They looked like fierce warrior women and were hidden by a veil deep within this rainforest; along with all the secrets of the universe.

"This is beautiful," I said in complete amazement.

"This *was* beautiful," the voice replied glumly.

"What happened?"

"A lot of things. Everything has its cycle and those cycles are not only delegated to earth, but for all lifeforces within life itself."

As I looked to my left, there was now a woman standing next to me, replacing the mysterious figure that came with the voice; her face covered by a veil. Her piercing gray eyes reflected through the veil; like reflective owl eyes that penetrated the depth of one's soul, taking inventory of everything contained inside of you. Like the man with blue eyes, she also carried an ankh, and she wore a deep, blood-red crown.

She carried with her a large silver looking spear, with another golden spear tucked along her back. She was wearing a long, red dress that hung past her ankles, that had a black lace trim that went around the edges of it. It was paired with a long, golden robe. She wore a gold band on her wedding ring finger that had inscriptions all over it. Around her neck was a necklace made of gold that held a heart shaped locket with an emerald jewel in the center of it.

She began to thrust her arms toward the sky, her robe becoming one with her body, turning into wings. Both wings were bigger than she was; one was white and the other black. Grabbing my hand, we took flight towards the sky, which then became the utter blackness of deep space. Within this blackness, nothing penetrated through it. There were no stars, moons, planets, or anything else within this blackness. It was nothing but a hallow abyss.

"Do you hear that?" She asked, letting go of my hand. Her voice was deep and low-pitched.

I listened for a sound; any sound of any kind, but there was nothing at all to be heard other than crisp, clear buzzing silence.

"I don't hear anything at all," I replied moments later, confused by her question.

"How do you feel right now, being here–no sound, just silence, just us?"

"Even though you are here with me, I feel alone. All alone."

"All great things are made in this darkness; through an intricate process of creation. The light alters the effect of this process and, in some cases, can destroy the creation being made itself. Light and dark are both bringers of life and death, beginnings, and endings.

Both energies are needed for the development process; similarly, to what film goes through while being developed in a darkroom."

She spoke with such grace and eloquence; taking her time to connect each dot with detailed analysis. I could tell there were many sides to her; one sides I could see was slightly playful while the another was of pure wisdom and intellect. Each word she spoke seemed to be encrypted with a special kind of magic that brought each word to life.

"I have seen many things over time, observed, and learned so much more through mankind alone. Mankind has searched often and often came up empty; looking for the answers outside of themselves, like little children. But I have always been here. I AM always here and will always be here. I AM inside of every living organism known to humanity, including humanity itself. This concept seems too complex for most to understand, while others seem to not only understand, but flourish within its magnificence.

"I knew since the beginning of time when I created this universe and everything within it, that with every beginning would be an end. This saddened me. I did not want it to end. I wanted to experience all things and all things to experience me, forever. So, I created multiple universes all within the same image – to be operated the same, governed the same, love the same, hate the same, *be* the same.

"With this creation also came the creation of gods and goddesses – divine and impartial beings that could hear mankind's prayers with the ability to intervene on behalf of them. All acting as many operators within one central operating network. I AM known by many names – none of them are accurate. These were all mankind's feeble attempts to explain the unexplainable. I AM something you cannot define by words, thoughts, or feelings. I AM all that I AM. I AM all that you are."

Suddenly, we arrived at a place in space where planets were crashing into each other. There were bright balls of fire being tossed from one side to the other. Planets and moons were exploding into millions of pieces all over the place. It was complete chaos! There were pieces of debris hurled everywhere, creating mass destruction. Once the chaos ended, there was complete silence. There were no longer any stars, planets, or moons. Only the abyss remained, until there was a spark that lit up in the background.

"This spark you see in the back is what constructed the universe as you now know it. I took this spark and created the most beautiful gift of life this universe has ever known; birthing her through the biggest cosmic flare this universe had ever seen. I decided to place her in the pure, holy place of Nibiru, where she would grow and learn more about her true nature.

The scene began to emerge, depicting the Holy place of Nibiru. She continued,

"I delivered her in a hand-woven basket and took her to the Holy place of Nibiru. I lie her beside the still Holy Waters. She was given as a gift of purity; one of pure creation. Little did the people of Nibiru know, this gift of magnificent creation would eventually become the creator of all creations. As a little girl, she grew up being raised to the ways and customs of the fierce, strong, and pure Priestesses of the holy land.

"They trained daily for battle, practicing various strategic moves and tactics; as they were among the first to be disbursed in battle within the holy land. They were revered, they were fierce, and they were deeply loved and cherished amongst their people. They were entrusted with the protection, purity, and blessings of their people; raising her in their image.

"She was raised by the Queen of the Priestesses as her own, with the other Priestesses being well-advised to never speak the truth of the little girl's origins to her. The little girl watched the ways of the Priestesses; how they operated and displayed pureness and unconditional love for all, taking integrity in everything they touched.

"She loved the Priestesses and modeled herself after them, especially the one she was most fond of, her name was Pallas. Pallas was the sister of the Queen Priestess and spent the most time with the little girl. Against the orders of her Queen priestess sister, Pallas would allow the little girl to practice fighting tactics and strategies, often offering additional skilled combat training only a select few of the Priestesses had.

"Pallas paid special attention to the little girl because she knew she was far greater than anything any of the Priestesses were or had ever been. The universe blessing the Priestesses with this beautiful child was taken with deep gratitude, especially by Pallas herself. She took the little girl under her wing the moment she began walking and she prepared her for all potential angles of the journey that was ahead of her.

"The two were inseparable. Until one horrible day when an attempt was made to destroy the pure, holy place of Nibiru. This attempt was almost successful. War was waged upon the priestesses by a dark force, managing to dismantle the Priestesses and the holy and pure place of Nibiru. At the first sign of this war, Pallas told the little girl to hide in a brush of leaves and not to come out, no matter what she saw.

"The little girl did as she was told and watched the battle ensue. The Priestesses were completely helpless against this magnitude of dark energy. This resulting in the Priestesses being slain all over the Holy land, right before the little girl's very eyes. After watching the brutality and severity of the events that had taken place, she decided she could no longer remain in hiding and began to emerge from the brushes she was hidden away in.

"Pallas saw the little girl coming out of the brush, and to stop her, she began running towards the little girl. However, upon running to the little girl, she was hit by an explosion that went off next to the area the little girl was headed to. The explosion blew Pallas's body into bits right in front of the little girl's face, stopping her dead in her tracks. In complete shock and horror, she dropped to her knees. It felt as if all the wind had been knocked right out of her.

"The little girl looked to her left and then her right. She looked in front, behind, and above her and only saw death. A few yards away lied her mother, the Queen, who was also slain gruesomely. The pain was too much for the little girl to bear. This ignited a switch within her that brought about a flame she could not put out. The pain had overtaken her to a point of no recognition and no return.

"Unable to fight the flame off anymore, she let out a shrill scream that brought everyone and everything on the Holy land, to their knees instantly. The once little girl then burst into flames, resembling that of a phoenix and a wolf. She then preceded to take everything into her fury of flames within the hundreds of miles that surrounded her, reducing everything that once was to ash.

"Her ashes and all the surrounding ashes of her city, people, and the hundreds of miles around it, all came together and formed who and what she is now – the Phoenix Wolf. She then went on for many, many eons observing, collecting, conquering, and then encumbering all the surrounding galaxies and everything that operated within it. As she began learning more about herself and the new universes that were now a part of her, she noticed a strange sensation within her that birthed the desire to create a new kind of universe of her own.

"A universe where she could observe, study, learn, experience, and become more aware about herself and who she is; testing her capabilities and limits within the realm of creation itself. She created this universe and everything within it with all that she is. A universe capable of not only creating new life but sustaining it, nurturing it, evolving it, and being able to watch it grow into infinite other creations. Extending beyond the reach of any perception, touching into infinity and beyond."

The black abyss began to shift into a planetary lineup of planets, moons, and stars, along with the space in between. It was once complete chaos, now turned into a beautiful symphony; a truly beautiful work of art. I peered into the chaos of creation and could also feel the eyes of the chaos of creation peering back into me. At that moment, we became one.

We were now operating as one, I was no longer an outsider looking in. I was now the insider looking out. I had an instant understanding of everything, including things I could never understand before. I felt everything she felt, saw everything she saw, and envisioned everything the way it is now. There were universal laws at play; laws that governed everything within the all, nothing being able to operate outside of the laws.

I went along as an observer on the journeys that brought all forms of life into becoming. I could see the beginning of time itself.

I was there for all the trials and tribulations; all the happiness and glory associated with this journey of creation. The making of the universe, the galaxies, the planets housed within it, the stars, moons, and all of the space that was in between. The journey of time. The journey of creation. The journey of birth, life, pain, and death.

Suddenly reappearing in view, she turned to me and asked, "It's beautiful, isn't it?"

"It is. All endings become new beginnings. All old things become new again." I responded, in complete wonderment.

"Precisely. Nothing ever dies; it goes on to become more of what it already is."

"Beautiful. Just beautiful."

Feeling a tear fall from my eye, I felt honored to be a part of this moment. Being able to take this information in through an un-filtered lens, without it being regurgitated with several redactions. Taken in from a firsthand experience rather than a cultivated per-spective. It was poetic in many more forms than one. Nothing could put into words the complete euphoria I was feeling at this moment. Wiping the tear from my eye, she then said,

"I am going to show you why you are here - why you have been called upon. Everything is always beautiful in the beginning, but as the little girl learned at an early age - all good and beautiful things have an end also. Those endings then go on to create new begin-nings, but they inevitably put an end to the good things one once had. You must understand the very beginning and the things that transpired to fully understand what must be done."

We were then brought to a time when the Holy Place of Nibiru and Earth were merged as one. There was only happiness and light - the darkness did not exist. There was the father of all lifeforces, who became known as the divine Universal Mind. This divine Universal Mind then created a son, a son that was created in His image.

"This son was taught the rules and laws that operated the universe and everything within it. Once the son had demonstrated comprehension, the son came to the father and asked him if he could also be a creator within this universe. The father was happy at this request and indulged his son.

"He eventually gave him the ability to rule and to create on his plane; while also giving him direct and explicit instruction on the rules and laws that governed all creation, as all light and life belong to the father. The son, now having his own plane to create, was still not satisfied and began to peer into the other realms, breaking many laws the father had instilled within him since birth.

"Consumed by greed, the son was no longer observing his father's laws regarding creation. After a while, the darkness manifested by the son created a rift between him and the father, as they represented two different things; one representing light and life, and the other representing the darkness and death.

"In attempt to reconcile things, the father searched for the son but the son became fearful and disillusioned. He refused to come out of where he was hiding. Until one fateful day when the son approached the father after being hiding for quite some time. The father, as always, welcomed his son. However, he began noticing his son was taking on an image of his own.

"The son approached the father and proceeded to demand his father's throne, stating he believed he was a better creator than his father. This caused a deep hurt and wound within the father, who no longer recognized the son whom he created in his image. The father, disheartened at his request, made the decision to separate the two created universes, allowing the son to become ruler of the darkness he created in his own image, within his own universe.

"Upon separating the two universes, a warning of the events that followed this separation was foretold. The father proceeded to tell the son that since he went against the laws and rules of creation, he must be held accountable for all his actions. He explained to his son again, that a creator of darkness can only create more of that resulting in death, decay, and rot; and therefore, cannot create anything that comes from the light.

"A creator of light creates all things resulting in life, love, and truth. The father then told the son that he would be held accountable for his actions in death; a death that will take away the son's immortality and cause pain for eternity, as no one escapes the law, including him. The consequence of his actions would ultimately result in him being swallowed by the same light and fire he desired so strongly to obtain, never again to see the light or any authority of it again.

"With that, the father also told his son to count the days as he would be returning soon. He would be returning to make all things new and to dissolve his entire universe the son had created under the disillusioned circumstances he created it within. The son laughed off his father's warnings and went back to ruling his plane, making a mockery of everything the father every created and everything the father stands for."

Time fast-forwarded, showing the chaos that erupted over time after the separation of the two worlds had been made. This chaos resulted in endless greed and a dark energy that was able to infiltrated mankind, brought in through the Babalon Working rituals. Since father gave humanity free will, he did not intervene in this matter; instead biding his time to make all things new again.

Multiple attempts of godly intervention from various sources were made, all to control and maintain the balance of light and dark. Some interventions included floods, fires, volcanoes, hurricanes, earthquakes, and famine, along with other various methods used to subdue the damage done to earth. After the multiple attempts were made to control and maintain the balance of light and dark; a decision was made that no more intervention from the gods and goddesses would be made.

It was decided that humanity, now partly created in the son's image and partly created in God's image, would stand, and face the fruits of their labors. Over time, the darkness grew and grew until the darkness began to drown out the light. The truth about the father was so deeply hidden from humanity; obscuring information, making it more and more difficult for humanity to reach the father.

In losing contact with the father, they lost contact with their true natures. This became displayed through the events that took place on Earth when the intervention became no more. There were wars within every country, family, and friendship - everything losing balance and harmony. Nothing being in balance and everything becoming chaos. With humanity losing contact with its primary creator, it lost contact with the truth and primary power within humanity itself.

Multiple evils were unleashed upon the earth. This created complete havoc with not only humanity itself but also with the natural resources, and other life forms housed on earth as well. As the time progressed, the dark energy began mutating into something far more progressed. Something that in due time would dismantle the entire universes altogether.

Looking at all the chaos that had overtaken Earth; wars that killed off so many innocent lives all for the greed of territory, and wickedly dark beliefs, it pained me to see something that was once so beautiful and created with such an enormous amount of thought and love, all being destroyed. I knew exactly what had to be done, but could not get the words to come out of my mouth. All I could feel was a ball in the back of my throat from all the tears I was trying to hold back.

We were projected back to the Royal Throne through an opening within the clouds on the ceiling. However, this time when we returned, we were accompanied by an audience. An audience of faces all familiar to me, but nameless. They were seated in their rightful seats circling the clouds at the top of the ceiling.

"What is this?" I turned and asked her.

"Your orders," she replied, her eyes gleaming through her dark veil, like little lights in a dark sky.

We moved towards the center of the throne. Below I could hear rumblings of voices whispering off in separate chatter amongst the room. Once we made it to the center of the throne, everyone stood to their feet and the room was immediately silenced.

"She has returned home!" She said, taking my hand and lifting it with hers.

The room filled with a roar of applause.

"You have all been given an invitation to witness a glorious event, an event that will bring many changes to us all! We are embarking on a journey that will establish a new beginning of time."

She then took my hand and faced me.

"You have been chosen, my child. You are to assimilate the Indygos and prepare them for the battles ahead. All your steps have always been pre-arranged, backed, guided, and supported by the divine Universal Mind because all your steps have been preparing you for this very moment and task. You must take this truth and enlighten the other Indygos. Tell them it is time and I AM coming.

"My children will know who you are and that you speak the truth. You will serve as my spokeswoman, the chosen intermediary between life itself, and the divine Universal Mind. It will serve you well to remember that love and the truth will always conquer all and is also the alchemist's ultimate form of alchemy in war. It can transmute even the darkest of energies and holds within it the power of the entire universe.

"Do you accept the powers given to you with the authority of the righteousness of the divine Universal Mind?"

Falling to my feet in complete reverence, I replied, "It would be my absolute honor."

Another roar of applause came from the gods and goddesses who were witnesses to this event. A green vine began emerging center of her palm. She pulled my hand closer and tighter to hers; her vine entering through the center of my palm, traveling throughout my body, intertwining itself throughout. The energy from the vine lifted me, continuing to surge with power until I was completely consumed.

I floated there, suspended in the air, rising through the same portal that opened in the ceiling, until I reached a place of nothing but clouds. It was completely quiet here and utterly peaceful. I knew I had been placed somewhere, somewhere that was preparing me for what was to come. An inner voice began speaking inside of me,

"Be wary of all who approach you in the time to come ahead. Some know the truth of who you are and look to weaken and distract your efforts. Your internal compass will guide you along the way, and I will be with you every step of the way. You are blessed. You are loved. You are protected. You are the enlightened one; you are to share this enlightenment with the world.

"Do not be afraid for I am always with you and could never leave your side. When you seek rest, I will provide. When you seek justice, I will provide. When you feel as though you cannot carry on, I will carry you the rest of the way. We will operate as one going forward. We are now one. We will move and operate as one thought, one word, and one single action.

"We will bring enlightenment and the life of the light to the world. I want you to tell my people about me and how much I love them. Tell them how I never left them, I have always been here, am here now, and will always be here. Even in the darkest of days to come, you will still find my people bringing enlightenment and the life of light to this world. My truth is one that cannot be ignored, one that cannot be lived without, and one that will defeat anything that stands in its way!

"The truth is here and is here to stay; with all once old things will become new again. There is more that is unseen, than is seen. This unseen force exists within all of humanity, it need only be awakened. The same way they live in me, I live in them. The battles ahead are not battles of man, they are battles of above and below. Tell all of humanity the truth of what you have seen, the truth of what you have felt. Go and tell my people to prepare themselves; for the Alpha, the Omega, the first, and the last is here. I AM that I AM.

"Let the battle begin!"

*****